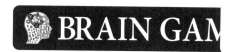

BRAIN GAM

MW00636184

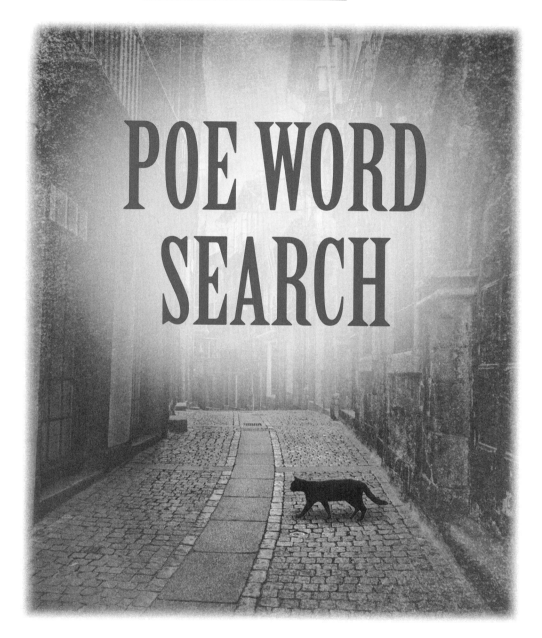

POE WORD
SEARCH

Publications International, Ltd.

Puzzle Creators: Ian Feigle and Nicole Sulgit

Puzzle Illustrator: Eric Biel

Brain Games is a registered trademark of Publications International, Ltd.

Louis Weber, CEO
Publications International, Ltd.
8140 Lehigh Avenue
Morton Grove, IL 60053

ISBN: 978-1-64030-671-4

Manufactured in U.S.A.

8 7 6 5 4 3 2 1

UNCOVER THE MYSTERY

Edgar Allan Poe was a groundbreaking literary figure of the American 1800s. As one of the first American writers to attempt to make his living from writing alone, Poe was well known in his time for his prose, poetry, and literary criticism, but today we know him for his macabre and morose stories. Tales like "The Tell-Tale Heart" and "The Black Cat" and poems like "The Raven" are so packed full of vivid imagery and literary cunning that they have had lasting influence on American culture, making his name synonymous with the gothic and murder-mystery genres of literature. And now, the mystery continues with *Brain Games®: Poe Word Search*, a page-turning puzzle book that adds another layer to be solved in Poe's work.

In *Brain Games®: Poe Word Search*, you'll find a large selection of word search puzzles that draw from some of Poe's most famous work. Scan the grids of letters with a critical eye to find key words that highlight the themes of Poe's work. If the puzzle's mystery is too difficult for you to crack, you can always find the answer key in the back of the book to help you solve it. Unlike many of Poe's murder-mystery tales whose murderers are so racked with guilt that they can't help but confess to their crimes, these puzzles are steadfast in their secrets and will not reveal their answers unless you put in the work. So grab a pencil and brace yourself for the thrilling series of puzzles that are in the pages to follow.

EDGAR ALLAN POE

Every word listed is contained within the group of letters. Words can be found in a straight line horizontally, vertically, or diagonally. They may be read either forward or backward.

AMONTILLADO

"ANNABEL LEE"

ARTHUR GORDON PYM

"THE BALLOON-HOAX"

CRYPTOGRAPHY

DETECTIVE FICTION

DUPIN

"EUREKA"

GOTHIC

HOUSE OF USHER

"LENORE"

MACABRE

MASQUE

NEVERMORE

PIT

POETRY

PENDULUM

PURLOINED

RED DEATH

"THE RAVEN"

ROMANTICISM

"TAMERLANE"

"THE TELL-TALE HEART"

"TO HELEN"

VIRGINIA CLEMM

WRITER

```
R H P I D H T A E D D E R X T A G G M
E S O I A O F R K W E L T I H O A L K
T Y E W I X I B D K T W P R T G W U X
I E T H E T E L L T A L E H E A R T T
R U R I S A V I R G I N I A C L E M M
W R Y J W Z F E R B A C A M O Y L A X
E E L L E B A N N A X M A Y D M E T J
E K O J F H X Y K S C N U U L Q N H C
N A N E L E H O T I M M V L U X O E W
A R O M A N T I C I S M I C U X R R O
L X A O H N O O L L A B E H T D E A K
R V G P U R L O I N E D Y K N P N V P
E Q P N O I T C I F E V I T C E T E D
M Q P O F M P E H D T S J F T S Q N P
A U O W A U Y H O U S E O F U S H E R
T T Y S L U C R Y P T O G R A P H Y B
S A Q R A R J H T I N E V E R M O R E
A U U K Y Q A M O N T I L L A D O E R
E A R T H U R G O R D O N P Y M Y S I
```

Answers on page 172

THEMES AND GENRES

Every word listed is contained within the group of letters. Words can be found in a straight line horizontally, vertically, or diagonally. They may be read either forward or backward.

ADVENTURE

AFTERLIFE

ALCOHOLISM

BETRAYAL

CRYPTOGRAPHY

DARK ROMANTICISM

DEATH

DECOMPOSITION

DETECTIVE

HORROR

LOSS

MOURNING

PHRENOLOGY

PHYSIOGNOMY

POETRY

PREMATURE BURIAL

PSEUDOSCIENCE

REVENGE

SCIENCE FICTION

TORTURE

```
F  H  S  O  D  E  C  O  M  P  O  S  I  T  I  O  N
S  C  I  E  N  C  E  F  I  C  T  I  O  N  Z  J  Z
P  L  P  C  R  Y  P  T  O  G  R  A  P  H  Y  C  P
H  T  A  E  D  O  R  O  R  R  O  H  A  R  X  Z  S
L  M  J  B  X  U  W  G  O  Q  H  O  F  N  M  Y  E
E  E  Y  F  B  E  C  N  M  H  W  X  T  E  H  M  U
X  G  U  T  B  O  D  I  Q  S  D  J  E  V  S  O  D
X  I  N  A  D  V  E  N  T  U  R  E  R  I  B  N  O
S  T  A  E  N  W  Q  R  D  L  A  X  L  T  E  G  S
Y  X  M  L  V  U  O  U  U  G  S  O  I  C  T  O  C
O  W  O  L  O  E  Y  O  Y  T  H  A  F  E  R  I  I
L  X  O  B  Q  N  R  M  R  O  R  I  E  T  A  S  E
W  S  Y  X  B  Z  S  W  C  A  J  O  A  E  Y  Y  N
S  P  H  R  E  N  O  L  O  G  Y  P  T  D  A  H  C
Y  R  T  E  O  P  A  B  Q  B  Q  F  X  C  L  P  E
S  E  D  A  R  K  R  O  M  A  N  T  I  C  I  S  M
P  R  E  M  A  T  U  R  E  B  U  R  I  A  L  Z  I
```

Answers on page 172

THE POE FAMILY

Every word listed is contained within the group of letters. Words can be found in a straight line horizontally, vertically, or diagonally. They may be read either forward or backward.

ABANDONMENT

ACTORS

BOSTON

CONSUMPTION

COUNTY CAVAN

DAVID POE JR

DAVID POE SR

DEATH

EDGAR POE

FOSTER HOME

IRISH

MASSACHUSETTS

NEW ENGLAND

ROSALIE POE

SECOND

TROUPE

WILLIAM POE

```
A J I I A M T J D F R H A A B C K
B H K W C B A B M J S S E C O N D
A B S C Q M A P E I E Y P N S E N
N Y T V X I D O R O I B S T D W N
D E M X W R P I P E D U T G S E T
O O W N B D E E O A M E A X R N H
N G L X I A I P V P S R J R O G T
M O F V F L M I T U P F H B T L A
E V A M A A D I H O Z T B K C A E
N D I S I P O C E T M N A T A N D
T B O L O N A R R B J D N Z M D F
K R L E H S K O T C P D L X T X C
D I S N S K U I B O S T O N X B G
W R T A S P N P J R H G B Y E P I
G R M I E F I Y F D T B O L G Y Y
C O U N T Y C A V A N D E V L Y R
Z F O S T E R H O M E V B F Q Q L
```

Answers on page 172

WILLIAM HENRY LEONARD POE

Every word listed is contained within the group of letters. Words can be found in a straight line horizontally, vertically, or diagonally. They may be read either forward or backward.

ABANDONED

ALCOHOLISM

AUTHOR

BALTIMORE

BROTHER

CARETAKER

CLERK

"DREAMS"

FRIGATE

MEDITERRANEAN

"ORIGINAL"

POET

RICHMOND

RUSSIA

SAILOR

SEAFARER

SOUTH AMERICA

"THE PIRATE"

TRAVELLER

TUBERCULOSIS

USS *MACEDONIAN*

VIRGINIA

WEST INDIES

```
Z  I  B  A  C  I  R  E  M  A  H  T  U  O  S  Y  R
U  A  C  L  N  A  I  N  I  G  R  I  V  Y  J  E  E
X  J  E  A  B  A  N  D  O  N  E  D  V  O  L  T  H
E  R  W  E  S  T  I  N  D  I  E  S  X  L  E  S  T
K  R  P  V  U  H  Y  N  L  I  U  G  E  O  I  Z  O
A  F  O  R  G  N  N  A  O  K  L  V  P  S  V  F  R
K  P  H  M  R  R  N  V  D  D  A  L  O  O  F  Z  B
M  F  O  R  I  I  O  R  P  R  E  L  N  R  A  B  U
S  N  G  A  G  T  E  H  T  E  U  C  I  Z  R  O  P
I  W  S  I  M  A  L  W  T  C  K  G  A  M  H  V  E
L  R  R  R  M  J  U  A  R  U  A  J  U  M  A  I  I
O  O  U  S  P  X  R  E  B  T  A  R  U  S  S  I  A
H  L  C  F  W  I  B  H  E  L  G  D  L  U  N  S  B
O  I  Q  L  P  U  L  D  N  O  M  H  C  I  R  V  U
C  A  R  E  T  A  K  E  R  S  E  L  W  G  R  E  V
L  S  H  J  N  A  E  N  A  R  R  E  T  I  D  E  M
A  T  F  R  K  W  N  L  N  R  E  R  A  F  A  E  S
```

Answers on page 172

ELIZABETH ARNOLD HOPKINS POE

Every word listed is contained within the group of letters. Words can be found in a straight line horizontally, vertically, or diagonally. They may be read either forward or backward.

ACTRESS

BOARDING HOUSE

BOSTON

CHARLES HOPKINS

CHARLES TUBBS

CHARLESTON COMEDIANS

DAVID POE JR.

EDGAR

ELIZA

LONDON

MARRIED

MOTHER

MR. EDGAR

NEW ENGLAND

NORFOLK

ROSALIE

SPITTING BLOOD

THEATER TROUPE

TRAVELLING

VIRGINIA

WIDOW

WILLIAM

YELLOW FEVER

```
C H A R L E S T O N C O M E D I A N S
J C W Z R S B B U T S E L R A H C C K
B S D G O F D O O L B G N I T T I P S
O H A R S O C K V R T P M Q L H Z Y N
A A V E A E M Y M R M R M N Y S S T I
R I I F L W V P E E E E D E D G A R K
D D D J I P D V O N P V A S P R I R P
I B P D E A I G O N U E Y D C T C X O
N E O Q U Z D D U M O F M N E R F C H
G W E T W Z N S N H R W I A L A L B S
H V J M L O C C K B T O N L Y V P B E
O M R M L E X G O X R L O G K E S E L
U A A R O W L S K Q E L R N G L F G R
S I C E D T T I J S T E F E L L P N A
E L T D J O H K Z O A Y O W D I B O H
E L R G N F X E K A E X L E S N V J C
C I E A U M S J R J H A K N I G X V J
M W S R K H M V R W T A I N I G R I V
I G S M A R R I E D H Z E J S X O J A
```

Answers on page 173

13

DAVID POE JR.

Every word listed is contained within the group of letters. Words can be found in a straight line horizontally, vertically, or diagonally. They may be read either forward or backward.

ABANDONED FAMILY

ACTOR

BALTIMORE

BOSTON

DAVID POE SR.

EDGAR

ELIZA

ELIZABETH CAIRNES

FATHER

ILL-TEMPERED

LAWYER

MARYLAND

MASSACHUSETTS

NEW YORK

NORFOLK

ROSALIE

STAGE FRIGHT

THEATER TROUPE

UNKNOWN FATE

WILLIAM

```
P  B  G  T  R  N  E  W  Y  O  R  K  G  E  R  D  E
Q  D  Y  C  H  E  O  S  P  W  O  O  H  G  W  E  T
D  N  R  L  E  E  H  N  E  I  R  A  O  N  M  R  A
U  A  R  G  I  R  A  T  E  I  L  A  S  O  R  E  F
S  L  V  X  O  M  O  T  A  C  W  A  P  R  W  P  N
T  Y  D  I  V  A  A  M  E  F  I  C  C  F  D  M  W
T  R  A  R  D  E  T  F  I  R  U  T  H  O  Y  E  O
E  A  Z  A  F  P  C  H  D  T  T  O  E  L  N  T  N
S  M  N  G  C  S  O  E  G  E  L  R  C  K  A  L  K
U  K  L  D  M  J  K  E  W  I  N  A  O  Y  F  L  N
H  T  M  E  C  R  F  I  S  K  R  O  B  U  J  I  U
C  P  D  Q  X  G  L  R  D  R  E  F  D  U  P  Q  X
A  M  C  Z  S  L  D  Y  Y  P  Y  A  E  N  Y  E  X
S  G  Y  W  I  E  C  W  L  Y  W  G  Z  G  A  A  F
S  W  R  A  K  C  X  W  E  G  A  K  E  I  A  B  Q
A  Q  M  B  O  S  T  O  N  L  L  O  C  W  L  T  A
M  E  L  I  Z  A  B  E  T  H  C  A  I  R  N  E  S
```

Answers on page 173

VIRGINIA ELIZA CLEMM POE

Every word listed is contained within the group of letters. Words can be found in a straight line horizontally, vertically, or diagonally. They may be read either forward or backward.

BALTIMORE

CONTROVERSIAL

FIRST COUSIN

FORDHAM

FRANCES SARGENT OSGOOD

HONEYMOON

MAJOR INFLUENCE

MARIA POE

MARRIED

MARYLAND

MISSED EDUCATION

NEW YORK

NEW YORK CITY

SIS

SISSY

THE BRONX

THIRTEEN

TUBERCULOSIS

UNDERAGE

WESTMINSTER HALL

WIFE

WILLIAM CLEMM JR.

```
U C U D J Y A E G A R E D N U P H N F L C
W E S T M I N S T E R H A L L Z B A W A M
P T U Y C N E W Y O R K C I T Y J L F I H
H H O N E Y M O O N Q N V S I S S Y V S R
M I S S E D E D U C A T I O N I O O B R L
S I S O L U C R E B U T A Z Q M H L P E H
E B W F O R D H A M H M A R Y L A N D V Z
S V E S H A E J R E N A X C A Z H A D O C
M D Q D I C W B B I H Q W T G E R E J R F
W G J X J S N R S L R M C Q I C I I F T S
W U X T A C O U V X A H O F O R E V Z N S
L K R X T N O T I X H N I K R O F O K O C
N Z J B X C T Q J W F U S A P T Z L I C V
H E D C T R J M M E L C M A I L L I W Q N
U S E S Q Y Z Z N Y O I E I M K M N Y K
Z A R T V C G R Y M X R J W B A B V H R L
Y I A E R O M I T L A B V K C O N S O L X
F G A U M I Z N B M E X C L Y Y F Y R V M
I E F I W X H D A M W G Y V W X W T I T L
R D O O G S O T N E G R A S S E C N A R F
M A J O R I N F L U E N C E N B V D W X V
```

POE'S UPBRINGING WITH THE ALLANS

Every word listed is contained within the group of letters. Words can be found in a straight line horizontally, vertically, or diagonally. They may be read either forward or backward.

ANCIENT LANGUAGES

BAPTIZED

DEBTS

DROPOUT

EDGAR ALLAN

ENGAGEMENT

ENGLAND

EPISCOPAL CHURCH

FOSTER HOME

GAMBLING

GRAMMAR SCHOOL

HENRI LE RENNET

HONOR GUARD

IRVINE

JOHN ALLAN

LIEUTENANT

LONDON

MERCHANT

ODD JOBS

RICHMOND

SAIL

SARAH ROYSTER

SCOTLAND

SCOTTISH

VIRGINIA

C N E P I S C O P A L C H U R C H
V O H E N R I L E R E N N E T Y W
O D N A L G N E V H N K Y M T O X
M N H W L O O H C S R A M M A R G
L O J P O D D O V I R G I N I A G
R L E K D N E N Z T H H S A N N M
E E N E D A Z O Z T Q X B L I T T
T D G Q J L I R B O F P I L N N U
S G A F O T T G A C B Q B A A M O
Y A G B B O P U Z S Y M H N I W P
O R E E S C A A N K A C E H X N O
R A M N Q S B R Z G R T S O Q D R
H L E I Y S M D U E U B K J Q W D
A L N V S A I L M E W D E B T S C
R A T R N F E O I D N O M H C I R
A N C I E N T L A N G U A G E S G
S V L F O S T E R H O M E N D R W

Answers on page 173

POE'S MILITARY CAREER

Every word listed is contained within the group of letters. Words can be found in a straight line horizontally, vertically, or diagonally. They may be read either forward or backward.

A BOSTONIAN

ARTIFICER

ARTILLERY

BOSTON HARBOR

CHARLESTON

DISCHARGED

ENLISTED

FIRST PUBLICATION

FORT INDEPENDENCE

FORT MOULTRIE

RECONCILIATION

SERGEANT MAJOR

SOUTH CAROLINA

TAMERLANE

TWO YEARS

UNDERAGE

WALTHAM

```
N E C N E D N E P E D N I T R O F
O U J Z E N A L R E M A T M M N M
I E N L I S T E D D C I U T A O F
T D V S F E M H O Y B N R U P I L
A V V O O J A Z M R O O O N Q T R
C P F U R R O A E S T J D R A Y
I O J T T D X I H L T S A E E I Z
L R H H M D Z U T L O O M R C L M
B U W C O I T F L I N B T A I I O
U R R A U S W Y A T H A N G F C L
P D D R L C O V W R A L A E I N J
T Y J O T H Y C H A R L E S T O N
S E N L R A E E Q N B M G V R C P
R S M I I R A Z X S O W R P A E J
I B E N E G R B W P R S E G X R X
F P G A F E S I A Z M X S V M N R
C U N G A D T G B N B U J C Y R U
```

POE'S DISCHARGE FROM THE MILITARY

Every word listed is contained within the group of letters. Words can be found in a straight line horizontally, vertically, or diagonally. They may be read either forward or backward.

AL AARAAF

BALTIMORE

COURT MARTIALED

DISMISSAL

DISOBEDIENCE

DISOWNED

ELIZABETH POE

GROSS NEGLECT

MARIA CLEMM

MATRICULATED

MILITARY ACADEMY

NEW YORK

POEMS

QUARRELS

REPLACED

VIRGINIA CLEMM

WEST POINT

WIDOWED AUNT

```
V  I  R  G  I  N  I  A  C  L  E  M  M  W  M  K  C
M  K  T  U  A  B  M  R  S  U  P  B  S  A  X  M  R
I  K  B  O  L  D  H  L  C  D  K  G  I  J  A  C  T
L  T  N  U  A  D  E  W  O  D  I  W  I  T  L  N  D
I  E  D  S  A  R  H  C  N  A  D  S  R  Q  I  F  I
T  M  S  B  R  C  B  I  A  I  Z  I  O  O  C  Y  S
A  N  X  A  A  I  B  A  S  L  C  P  P  W  W  R  O
R  N  U  Z  A  M  M  M  L  U  P  T  R  G  N  I  B
Y  Q  L  W  F  A  I  N  L  T  S  E  F  K  G  E  E
A  C  L  L  S  S  E  A  E  E  I  O  R  G  H  B  D
C  Z  S  N  S  W  T  E  W  B  P  M  S  E  H  F  I
A  B  G  A  Y  E  P  B  G  Q  M  O  O  F  G  H  E
D  J  L  O  D  E  A  V  K  U  E  N  E  R  S  D  N
E  Q  R  R  M  A  R  I  A  C  L  E  M  M  E  V  C
M  K  E  L  I  Z  A  B  E  T  H  P  O  E  S  B  E
Y  C  O  U  R  T  M  A  R  T  I  A  L  E  D  Q  K
T  C  E  L  G  E  N  S  S  O  R  G  P  J  P  C  T
```

Answers on page 174

POE'S PUBLISHERS

Every word listed is contained within the group of letters. Words can be found in a straight line horizontally, vertically, or diagonally. They may be read either forward or backward.

BALTIMORE SATURDAY VISITER

BROADWAY JOURNAL

BURTON'S GENTLEMAN'S MAGAZINE

EVENING MIRROR

GRAHAM'S MAGAZINE

SOUTHERN LITERARY MESSENGER

THE STYLUS

```
R  C  F  E  U  D  X  D  V  O  N  G  B  B  N  P  P  S  W  W  Y  W  W  G  P
E  N  L  N  C  F  T  I  V  R  D  Y  J  H  L  P  A  B  C  A  E  B  D  D  N
G  T  W  I  I  C  F  S  J  L  E  Q  U  U  B  B  P  J  U  V  F  A  Y  X  S
N  U  F  Z  Y  L  F  H  P  D  M  E  M  T  V  L  G  D  F  H  E  L  C  A  R
E  X  L  A  E  N  I  Z  A  G  A  M  S  M  A  H  A  R  G  X  R  T  S  N  Z
S  D  P  G  H  E  J  T  V  I  V  S  A  H  O  U  K  W  U  W  W  I  Y  R  P
S  G  P  A  D  O  R  D  T  U  C  W  Q  W  U  F  N  W  K  E  R  M  W  Y  S
E  B  O  M  R  A  A  O  F  U  U  H  R  D  V  F  B  S  K  C  P  O  Z  R  Z
M  M  E  S  D  C  Q  V  P  O  Y  A  L  Q  J  P  G  Q  Y  L  S  R  N  E  Q
Y  C  H  N  Z  H  X  V  V  K  R  T  C  U  K  S  F  R  Y  O  D  E  Q  Z  X
R  W  S  A  R  D  B  I  G  K  B  V  K  V  J  T  L  W  Y  K  Y  S  D  T  Z
A  K  O  M  K  C  L  R  T  U  Q  Y  E  B  K  L  Q  R  F  C  U  A  C  A  C
R  Q  F  E  U  Y  I  M  O  R  G  U  I  Y  A  Q  I  N  E  Q  L  T  O  N  B
E  W  Z  L  P  S  R  W  L  A  P  G  I  R  T  X  L  Q  S  J  U  U  U  L  L
T  H  B  T  P  E  Z  I  Y  W  D  B  T  X  X  Z  J  U  M  G  D  R  K  L  R
I  S  L  N  Z  P  C  I  U  N  Q  W  X  H  C  U  W  S  G  Y  H  D  N  P  O
L  G  V  E  O  A  B  N  T  D  K  O  A  W  E  W  G  A  Y  R  F  A  A  U  U
N  V  T  G  U  T  B  O  I  G  L  W  D  Y  J  S  K  Z  C  Q  J  Y  D  L  W
R  N  C  S  I  X  J  I  R  V  E  T  I  Z  J  U  T  I  U  M  S  V  X  N  A
E  V  E  N  I  N  G  M  I  R  R  O  R  T  R  O  V  Y  E  Q  F  I  C  H  J
H  T  Q  O  Q  V  W  C  E  U  S  A  U  M  R  H  U  W  L  S  J  S  M  S  F
T  P  G  T  S  U  R  M  F  E  M  L  M  U  H  N  J  R  H  U  F  I  L  R  K
U  U  K  R  Q  P  Y  C  E  P  N  K  Z  N  Z  Z  F  J  N  X  S  T  Q  V  G
O  T  L  U  R  H  P  L  Q  H  B  K  R  L  K  X  O  Z  V  A  N  E  N  C  H
S  F  N  B  Z  B  Z  W  O  S  L  O  B  B  W  H  F  H  X  U  L  R  T  Y  A
```

Answers on page 174

POE'S WRITING CAREER

Every word listed is contained within the group of letters. Words can be found in a straight line horizontally, vertically, or diagonally. They may be read either forward or backward.

"ANNABEL LEE"

AUTHOR

CRITIC

DETECTIVES

EDITOR

"ELDORADO"

"EULALIE"

FULL TIME

GOTHIC

HORROR

"HOP-FROG"

"LENORE"

"LIGEIA"

"MORELLA"

POET

PROFESSIONAL

SHORT STORIES

"THE BELLS"

"THE BLACK CAT"

"THE GOLD BUG"

"THE RAVEN"

"TO HELEN"

TOMAHAWK MAN

"ULALUME"

```
S  G  T  Z  T  T  W  V  W  A  F  N  X  H  E  C  G  N  O
E  S  E  I  R  O  T  S  T  R  O  H  S  M  S  R  O  E  T
D  E  T  N  F  R  S  N  R  A  E  R  U  M  C  M  T  V  H
O  E  O  E  B  E  D  B  F  I  L  L  R  T  U  C  H  A  E
H  L  M  L  L  M  E  E  S  M  A  L  E  O  W  Z  I  R  B
O  L  A  E  A  I  R  Z  T  L  O  M  E  I  T  K  C  E  E
P  E  H  H  N  T  G  G  U  E  X  Z  F  R  L  I  Z  H  L
F  B  A  O  O  L  I  U  D  Y  C  L  I  Y  O  A  D  T  L
R  A  W  T  I  L  U  Z  B  Y  Z  T  O  C  E  M  L  E  S
O  N  K  Y  S  U  C  C  E  D  A  O  I  J  T  T  A  U  K
G  N  M  A  S  F  Q  N  S  P  L  V  I  V  O  I  Q  Z  E
O  A  A  I  E  U  C  U  J  E  P  O  Y  S  E  O  O  B  O
U  H  N  K  F  P  E  K  L  S  E  A  G  G  A  S  C  J  E
Q  Z  T  Y  O  B  R  D  E  O  H  M  I  E  W  N  R  E  H
Z  Y  H  E  R  G  O  S  F  M  X  L  K  N  H  M  I  L  O
M  Q  T  D  P  R  N  R  R  O  H  T  U  A  Z  T  T  F  R
R  O  N  M  A  V  E  X  P  M  P  L  W  I  D  E  I  Q  R
H  C  H  D  K  S  L  B  F  H  Y  R  B  I  I  M  C  V  O
A  C  O  T  H  E  B  L  A  C  K  C  A  T  R  G  Z  K  R
```

Answers on page 174

POE'S POETRY

Every word listed is contained within the group of letters. Words can be found in a straight line horizontally, vertically, or diagonally. They may be read either forward or backward.

"A DREAM"

"A PAEAN"

"AL AARAAF"

"ALONE"

"AN ACROSTIC"

"DREAMS"

"ELIZABETH"

"EVENING STAR"

"FAIRY-LAND"

"IMITATION"

"ROMANCE"

"SONG"

"SPIRITS OF THE DEAD"

"STANZAS"

"TAMERLANE"

"THE HAPPIEST DAY"

"THE LAKE"

"TO HELEN"

"TO ISAAC LEA"

"TO MARGARET"

"TO SCIENCE"

"TO THE RIVER"

```
Y  O  P  T  A  M  E  R  L  A  N  E  P  N  C  Y  Z  T  X
A  B  M  Q  C  O  G  R  F  D  S  W  H  J  Z  Y  V  O  I
D  E  X  Q  V  H  Y  A  S  R  T  I  S  O  N  Z  T  M  V
T  E  Z  D  F  Y  A  T  M  U  B  J  S  T  A  N  Z  A  S
S  A  L  B  F  R  L  S  A  Q  C  F  A  D  Y  I  U  R  X
E  G  H  I  A  I  D  G  E  B  H  X  P  Z  G  A  E  G  Q
I  B  O  A  Z  U  M  N  R  C  H  Z  B  N  L  E  T  A  R
P  C  L  N  A  A  L  I  D  Z  H  G  A  O  Z  C  O  R  E
P  A  F  A  R  B  B  N  T  W  L  E  N  H  S  N  I  E  V
A  W  A  C  M  U  S  E  U  A  A  E  B  M  C  A  S  T  I
H  G  I  R  H  E  X  V  T  P  T  I  R  W  Z  M  A  W  R
E  N  R  O  L  K  T  E  A  H  Q  I  A  P  A  O  A  K  E
H  O  Y  S  O  A  W  O  O  L  V  V  O  D  W  R  C  R  H
T  S  L  T  H  L  E  G  H  K  M  G  S  N  R  P  L  A  T
N  Q  A  I  W  E  S  M  U  E  O  D  F  G  K  E  E  I  O
E  P  N  C  A  H  B  E  A  Z  L  R  H  N  C  F  A  D  T
H  A  D  Y  P  T  T  X  W  F  I  E  T  G  V  C  R  M  C
R  R  S  Y  U  Z  Z  W  B  U  E  C  N  E  I  C  S  O  T
T  W  S  P  I  R  I  T  S  O  F  T  H  E  D  E  A  D  V
```

Answers on page 175

POE'S POETRY PT. 2

Every word listed is contained within the group of letters. Words can be found in a straight line horizontally, vertically, or diagonally. They may be read either forward or backward.

"A VALENTINE"

"ANNABEL LEE"

"BRIDAL BALLAD"

"DEEP IN EARTH"

"ENIGMA"

"FANNY"

"FOR ANNIE"

"HYMN"

"ISRAFEL"

"LATIN HYMN"

"LINES ON JOE LOCKE"

"MAY QUEEN ODE"

"SERENADE"

"SPIRITUAL SONG"

"THE COLISEUM"

"THE RAVEN"

"THE SLEEPER"

"THE VALLEY OF UNREST"

"TO HELEN"

"TO ELIZABETH"

"TO MY MOTHER"

"TO ZANTE"

```
D  T  O  E  L  I  Z  A  B  E  T  H  O  X  Q  A  M  I  I
D  A  R  E  P  E  E  L  S  E  H  T  B  Y  U  V  S  E  D
J  S  L  G  V  J  J  D  H  S  C  E  D  Q  A  R  Y  F  W
H  P  I  L  L  B  T  L  P  S  E  R  E  N  A  D  E  K  K
H  I  N  J  A  Q  L  B  C  V  V  T  U  F  B  W  W  A  B
B  R  E  Q  T  B  J  F  M  P  O  I  E  C  I  X  N  N  T
E  I  S  M  I  J  L  G  J  H  T  L  P  G  L  W  U  N  O
N  T  O  F  N  Y  C  A  E  D  O  N  E  E  U  Q  Y  A  M
I  U  N  O  H  M  Q  L  D  H  Y  M  N  N  X  Y  E  B  Y
T  A  J  R  Y  W  E  V  L  I  K  F  A  I  A  T  H  E  M
N  L  O  A  M  N  T  D  O  J  R  D  K  K  N  Q  P  L  O
E  S  E  N  N  N  X  R  S  M  S  B  I  A  V  E  K  L  T
L  O  L  N  D  W  X  K  W  K  L  I  Z  G  L  C  E  E  H
A  N  O  I  F  C  N  O  I  Y  O  O  Q  S  N  R  U  E  E
V  G  C  E  H  E  L  S  A  X  T  C  B  T  E  G  T  U  R
A  Y  K  N  H  H  T  R  A  E  N  I  P  E  E  D  C  B  A
V  E  E  N  I  G  M  A  N  E  V  A  R  E  H  T  R  T  N
M  Y  N  N  A  F  T  H  E  C  O  L  I  S  E  U  M  E  Q
T  H  E  V  A  L  L  E  Y  O  F  U  N  R  E  S  T  T  A
```

Answers on page 175

POE'S TALES

Every word listed is contained within the group of letters. Words can be found in a straight line horizontally, vertically, or diagonally. They may be read either forward or backward.

"A PREDICAMENT"

"A TALE OF JERUSALEM"

"BERENICE"

"BON-BON"

"KING PEST"

"LIGEIA"

"LIONIZING"

"LOSS OF BREATH"

"METZENGERSTEIN"

"MORELLA"

"MYSTIFICATION"

"THE ASSIGNATION"

"WILLIAM WILSON"

```
Z  H  N  R  S  J  A  M  P  O  V  S  R  N  B  Q  X  M  H
S  T  O  N  U  H  P  R  M  F  I  I  T  C  E  E  X  E  L
G  A  S  D  O  R  H  A  X  R  U  T  V  L  U  L  J  L  U
W  E  L  F  E  B  Q  F  W  E  S  H  R  V  D  U  V  A  Z
T  R  I  O  R  U  N  B  V  E  R  J  H  D  T  M  M  S  Q
H  B  W  M  R  Y  L  O  P  J  N  P  D  B  I  Y  M  U  X
E  F  M  E  K  N  X  G  B  Z  K  T  E  L  S  Z  X  R  J
A  O  A  T  R  Q  N  S  N  I  K  R  Q  T  B  A  X  E  K
S  S  I  Z  V  I  T  P  J  A  E  P  I  L  F  P  K  J  M
S  S  L  E  K  Y  U  Y  J  N  L  F  P  H  Q  R  M  F  O
I  O  L  N  Y  T  H  E  I  F  I  I  V  M  G  E  O  O  R
G  L  I  G  C  A  X  C  P  C  M  I  G  Y  B  D  Q  E  E
N  W  W  E  C  M  E  V  A  I  J  M  S  E  B  I  L  L  L
A  C  O  R  P  A  V  T  F  H  Y  O  T  R  I  C  V  A  L
T  V  R  S  T  C  I  J  U  G  H  V  M  Y  E  A  H  T  A
I  W  O  T  O  O  G  D  C  P  P  Y  S  J  B  M  O  A  T
O  L  Q  E  N  O  M  L  U  R  R  O  N  U  M  E  P  R  M
N  E  L  I  O  N  I  Z  I  N  G  R  N  B  M  N  E  J  Y
T  G  G  N  M  E  E  R  G  Q  X  O  R  H  B  T  S  W  M
```

Answers on page 175

POE'S TALES PT. 2

Every word listed is contained within the group of letters. Words can be found in a straight line horizontally, vertically, or diagonally. They may be read either forward or backward.

"DIDDLING"

"ELEONORA"

"MELLONTA TAUTA"

"THE BLACK CAT"

"THE BUSINESS MAN"

"THE DEVIL IN THE BELFRY"

"THE GOLD-BUG"

"THE ISLAND OF THE FAY"

"THE MAN OF THE CROWD"

"THE OBLONG BOX"

"THE OVAL PORTRAIT"

"THE SPHINX"

"THE TELL-TALE HEART"

```
M  K  F  A  S  H  J  Y  Y  T  C  R  Q  R  K  T  T  V  Y
M  Q  T  R  C  L  G  E  W  O  E  E  J  U  R  Y  Y  T  R
E  N  H  O  O  K  T  H  E  B  L  A  C  K  C  A  T  H  F
L  T  E  N  T  P  P  W  D  Y  Y  Z  W  T  X  A  O  E  L
L  H  I  O  R  H  U  G  W  D  B  Z  H  N  D  R  Q  O  E
O  E  S  E  O  Z  E  Z  G  Z  Q  E  I  X  I  Y  F  V  B
N  T  L  L  R  L  Y  B  C  O  G  H  V  C  D  Y  B  A  E
T  E  A  E  Z  P  D  Y  U  O  P  L  N  Y  D  Q  S  L  H
A  L  N  B  J  X  V  Q  L  S  P  V  Q  O  L  F  M  P  T
T  L  D  F  E  O  F  D  E  D  I  Z  S  G  I  V  Y  O  N
A  T  O  W  M  A  B  H  L  O  A  N  V  U  N  C  D  R  I
U  A  F  X  F  U  T  H  I  M  W  T  E  D  G  L  Z  T  L
T  L  T  Q  G  N  E  I  I  F  Z  D  Z  S  W  T  D  R  I
A  E  H  C  Z  O  Y  M  K  O  J  F  F  Z  S  K  X  A  V
O  H  E  T  H  E  O  B  L  O  N  G  B  O  X  M  Y  I  E
U  E  F  L  K  Z  Y  Y  T  M  T  M  K  G  Y  W  A  T  D
M  A  A  N  G  Z  D  Q  B  H  O  R  M  W  M  O  L  N  E
T  R  Y  A  G  Q  J  Q  H  N  P  U  B  D  Q  W  H  B  H
W  T  H  E  M  A  N  O  F  T  H  E  C  R  O  W  D  F  T
```

Answers on page 175

35

POE'S TALES PT. 3

Every word listed is contained within the group of letters. Words can be found in a straight line horizontally, vertically, or diagonally. They may be read either forward or backward.

"LANDOR'S COTTAGE"

"MESMERIC REVELATION"

"SOME WORDS WITH A MUMMY"

"THE CASK OF AMONTILLADO"

"THE LANDSCAPE GARDEN"

"THE POWER OF WORDS"

"THE PURLOINED LETTER"

"THE PREMATURE BURIAL"

"THOU ART THE MAN"

"X-ING A PARAGRAB"

```
B  R  P  B  Q  F  D  E  K  V  G  B  X  O  U  E  W  G  L  A  Q
A  E  F  G  E  M  J  Q  E  U  M  N  C  C  D  P  F  C  Q  O  S
R  T  H  E  C  A  S  K  O  F  A  M  O  N  T  I  L  L  A  D  O
G  T  V  X  V  C  V  K  B  J  Z  F  Q  X  K  Y  X  D  G  G  L
A  E  J  N  Z  M  J  Q  J  B  F  T  L  K  X  N  X  A  E  N  R
R  L  Z  M  B  O  B  P  N  X  R  H  A  B  H  G  B  L  D  Y  Q
A  D  X  K  E  O  J  J  P  Q  F  C  N  G  C  T  J  Z  W  X  H
P  E  D  N  K  Z  D  U  K  U  F  D  D  P  D  H  E  X  B  Q  U
A  N  N  A  M  E  H  T  T  R  A  U  O  H  T  E  S  C  D  V  I
G  I  T  I  Q  O  P  J  U  B  C  P  R  O  R  P  S  Q  H  P  Q
N  O  Y  M  M  U  M  A  H  T  I  W  S  D  R  O  W  E  M  O  S
I  L  C  J  M  J  S  R  X  R  B  O  C  L  O  W  G  Z  U  P  L
X  R  L  R  T  Y  Q  G  Q  U  Y  W  O  X  B  E  M  Q  T  T  V
R  U  U  F  F  S  H  D  R  F  G  P  T  S  F  R  U  Y  H  E  W
G  P  Q  Q  A  K  Q  X  X  A  U  L  T  X  L  O  M  Z  K  K  W
O  E  P  E  L  D  H  H  X  Z  N  J  A  R  M  F  G  C  J  A  R
H  H  I  T  J  K  K  R  Q  U  Y  L  G  Z  T  W  F  H  E  B  H
R  T  H  P  N  N  H  Z  W  T  N  C  E  X  V  O  W  R  W  V  O
L  M  L  A  I  R  U  B  E  R  U  T  A  M  E  R  P  E  H  T  B
T  H  E  L  A  N  D  S  C  A  P  E  G  A  R  D  E  N  Y  L  R
N  O  I  T  A  L  E  V  E  R  C  I  R  E  M  S  E  M  Z  J  I
```

POE'S AGONY

Every word listed is contained within the group of letters. Words can be found in a straight line horizontally, vertically, or diagonally. They may be read either forward or backward.

ADDICTION

ALCOHOL

CHOLERA

DEAD MOTHER

DELIRIUM TREMENS

DEPRAVED

DEPRESSION

EPILEPSY

GAMBLING

GREAT DISTRESS

HEART DISEASE

MALIGNED

MENINGEAL INFLAMMATION

MOURNFUL

NO FATHER

OBITUARY

"POOR SOUL"

RABIES

"REYNOLDS"

RUFUS GRISWOLD

SLANDERED

SYPHILIS

TUBERCULOSIS

```
Y  L  R  S  C  H  N  H  C  M  P  S  R  E  Y  N  O  L  D  S  C
D  J  C  H  E  L  S  P  E  N  E  R  K  J  V  B  M  C  M  O  G
E  T  H  X  E  U  A  J  Q  G  R  E  S  Y  I  M  L  N  D  N  N
L  H  O  D  X  F  G  X  M  T  F  W  O  T  X  S  S  Y  F  W  O
I  D  L  T  R  N  B  A  D  A  L  X  U  P  L  X  I  L  P  U  I
R  J  E  H  U  R  P  V  M  O  L  A  O  A  Q  S  S  O  C  M  T
I  K  R  A  I  U  Y  N  H  B  R  I  N  A  Y  Z  O  W  W  D  C
U  G  A  U  D  O  D  O  Z  Y  L  D  G  P  B  R  L  J  P  L  I
M  H  R  K  A  M  C  N  T  N  E  I  H  N  S  B  U  N  K  O  D
T  N  E  E  H  L  O  G  S  R  O  I  N  O  E  C  C  Y  X  W  D
R  O  N  A  A  Y  B  T  E  M  L  I  U  G  M  D  R  S  R  S  A
E  F  L  N  R  T  S  D  H  I  A  L  S  B  X  R  E  P  A  I  A
M  A  W  B  F  T  D  J  S  E  B  O  E  S  X  U  B  E  B  R  Q
E  T  I  U  F  M  D  I  E  X  R  C  S  A  E  E  U  L  I  G  Z
N  H  N  Y  X  O  T  I  S  S  H  L  T  T  L  R  T  I  E  S  K
S  E  B  J  F  Y  B  O  S  T  K  O  S  G  P  F  P  P  S  U  G
N  R  R  Y  H  S  F  N  V  E  R  D  E  V  A  R  P  E  D  F  M
X  J  X  R  O  O  C  X  G  M  A  E  H  X  H  H  X  D  D  U  I
G  R  G  A  C  F  W  F  K  D  L  S  S  Y  P  U  Z  F  R  R  P
A  Q  I  X  X  D  Z  J  T  W  D  E  E  S  U  J  C  D  B  R  P
M  E  N  I  N  G  E  A  L  I  N  F  L  A  M  M  A  T  I  O  N
```

Answers on page 176

"THE PURLOINED LETTER"

Every word listed is contained within the group of letters. Words can be found in a straight line horizontally, vertically, or diagonally. They may be read either forward or backward.

ACQUAINTANCE
ASCENDANCY
ASSASSINATION
CASUAL
COINCIDENCE
CUNNING
DISCOMPOSED
GRASPED
HANDWRITING
IMAGINARY

INGENIOUS
JUXTAPOSITION
LIBRARY
LYNX EYE
MINISTER
MOTIONLESS
PARIS
PERFECT AGONY
PERFECTION
PERSEVERING
PHYSICIAN

PROFOUND
PURLOINED
RECOVERING
SELF EVIDENT
SILENCE
SIMPLE AND ODD
SPEECHLESS
SYMPTOMS
TREMBLING
WELCOME

```
J U L S N H Y D E S O P M O C S I D T T C
Y U C I I L P S H L D E H A A I I D L R O
O K X R B L G G V C N N S J I P F O E E I
H S W T S R E C U C L U U R X P B D V M N
M K S A A M A N M B A E I O I E I N I B C
T P P S C P O R C L P Z P G F E O A N L I
R R P G W Q O T Y E F H R M H O U E G I D
U E E P X A U S P C I K Y U G R R L E N E
D K M E Z A P A I M I P C S N T R P N G N
R S O R Y S U G I T Y R A N I G A M I L C
H D T F N C R N K N I S J V R C Y I O S E
A B I E O E L I E G T O J C E Q I S U P T
N U O C G N O N V Y J A N F V S Z A S E M
D T N T A D I N C U E N N H O W J W N E I
W W L I T A N U Q O L X N C C X H R N C N
R E E O C N E C S T Z Z N W E N I R V H I
I L S N E C D A I F N P J Y R P U W V L S
T C S R F Y E N Q N A I F Y L L B T J E T
I O P E R S E V E R I N G Y P B B H X S E
N M K V E N N O I T A N I S S A S S A S R
G E C O P F V S G Q S E L F E V I D E N T
```

Answers on page 176

"THE PURLOINED LETTER" PT. 2

Every word listed is contained within the group of letters. Words can be found in a straight line horizontally, vertically, or diagonally. They may be read either forward or backward.

ALLUDE

ANALOGOUS

CONCEALMENT

CONCERNING

CONVULSIONS

DELIBERATE

DISPUTE

EXECUTED

GIMLET

IDENTIFICATION

INGENUITY

INTELLECT

MAGNITUDE

NOVICE

OBVIOUS

OPPONENT

OVERSIGHT

PHYSICAL

PLACARDS

PROBING

PURLOINED

PUZZLES

REPUTATION

SCRUTINIZING

SCRUTINY

SIMPLETON

SNUFF BOX

SOUNDING

```
R U F T E L B G Y I G M Z H D H A K W Z S
Q Q G N T A C N Q D V N K M V Q L G Z K U
I S T E U C U I P A W O V J T V S N R I O
Q H L M P I Z Z P M X V G I M U F I P N I
D H I L S S J I R O D I I M O O S D L N V
T P F A I Y S N C D X C M G P U N N A I B
H U F E D H C I E Z K E O L E W O U C T O
G R D C V P R T C E L L E T N I I O A M X
I L E N Y W U U K M A N H J T Y S S R N O
S O L O H C T R T N S O J A W G L B D O N
R I I C E V I C A G N C C C R D U Q S T O
E N B X C L N S W W U I Y T V T V R E E I
V E E I M O Y H A P F G K C B N N G D L T
O D R P N S N Y B I F N Y H J E O W U P A
E V A P N G O C T X B G G J J N C B T M T
I U T U A Z E N E S O G N I B O R P I I U
C G E Z B L E N B R X E H R N P W V N S P
R E D Z P D L M U G N I B Q C P I Z G D E
Z B M L I F M U L I C I E N P O J A A G R
M U I E W U G B D W T L N B B T E L M I G
Z V U S H B A X I E A Y R G U U V S T D P
```

"THE PREMATURE BURIAL"

Every word listed is contained within the group of letters. Words can be found in a straight line horizontally, vertically, or diagonally. They may be read either forward or backward.

AGONY

ALL-ABSORBING

BROKEN

EMINENCE

ENDURED

EXPIRATION

EXTREMES

FEARFUL

GHASTLY

HORRIBLE

ILLUSTRIOUS

INFLAMED

INTENSE

INTERMETS

MAGIC PINIONS

PAINFUL

PORTALS

RESTORATIVES

REVIVED

SARCOPHAGUS

WIZARD WHEELS

```
H  I  N  T  E  R  M  E  T  S  Q  H  G  X  W  N  O  M  S
A  N  H  X  S  R  U  T  M  C  C  T  H  D  J  E  G  L  F
R  E  H  B  N  R  P  P  W  N  R  O  S  W  E  V  E  V  K
E  K  I  G  E  Q  E  B  Z  Q  Y  N  I  Y  F  E  D  E  E
S  O  U  B  T  V  J  V  C  X  O  R  G  S  H  Y  X  F  S
T  R  G  Z  N  Y  O  S  I  I  R  N  U  W  L  P  H  U  U
O  B  E  V  I  Q  E  K  N  V  I  E  D  X  I  M  O  K  G
R  F  Y  V  T  M  T  I  E  B  E  R  M  R  V  I  F  T  A
A  C  V  N  E  N  P  P  R  I  A  D  A  J  R  U  N  R  H
T  C  R  R  W  C  L  O  H  Z  Q  T  K  T  M  Y  Y  W  P
I  H  T  G  I  W  S  B  I  B  I  D  S  D  U  E  L  Y  O
V  X  H  G  D  B  V  W  K  O  V  U  B  E  H  N  U  E  C
E  U  A  A  A  G  X  Z  N  G  L  G  M  M  L  D  F  E  R
S  M  O  L  O  C  F  L  W  L  E  U  C  A  S  U  N  R  A
K  S  L  A  T  R  O  P  I  H  P  N  D  L  F  R  I  E  S
U  A  A  N  P  E  F  E  A  R  F  U  L  F  G  E  A  W  G
C  K  S  Y  L  T  S  A  H  G  R  R  K  N  M  D  P  B  V
S  R  Y  N  O  G  A  E  U  H  O  R  R  I  B  L  E  W  H
M  S  M  H  F  E  M  I  N  E  N  C  E  W  K  P  Q  R  O
```

Answers on page 177

"THE PREMATURE BURIAL" PT. 2

Every word listed is contained within the group of letters. Words can be found in a straight line horizontally, vertically, or diagonally. They may be read either forward or backward.

ABSOLUTE NIGHT
APPREHENSIONS
ASPHYTIC
AWFUL
BLACKNESS
CARELESSLY
CATALEPTIC
DANGER
DEATH
DESPAIR
DISORDER

ENTOMBED
ETERNAL
GALVANIC
INCIDENT
INDECENT HASTE
MEDICAL BOOKS
MORTAL TERRORS
OVERHEAD
PATIENT
PECULIARITY
POROUS

PRESERVATION
RECOVERY
REVIVED
SEPULTURE
SHRIEK
SQUEEZE
STRUGGLING
SUFFERER
THRILLING
TYPHUS FEVER
VIGILANCE

```
O  Y  P  G  N  E  D  L  Z  Q  W  Z  A  Y  M  J  H  M  U  C  G
R  I  A  P  S  E  D  B  F  A  P  W  P  Y  E  Q  V  C  R  I  N
V  Q  A  P  Z  L  B  A  C  K  Q  P  T  S  H  C  I  L  P  N  I
T  P  B  Q  C  O  Z  F  Q  D  Y  I  L  U  T  A  G  J  N  A  L
C  A  R  E  L  E  S  S  L  Y  R  J  E  O  M  T  I  F  W  V  L
S  T  W  N  P  A  C  P  T  A  E  T  E  R  N  A  L  E  E  L  I
I  I  S  F  V  R  D  X  I  H  S  Z  M  O  T  L  A  R  N  A  R
N  E  U  A  U  A  E  L  I  A  G  O  R  P  P  E  N  U  T  G  H
C  N  F  W  N  L  U  S  H  V  P  I  M  E  R  P  C  T  O  W  T
I  T  F  G  E  C  L  T  E  C  O  M  N  X  V  T  E  L  M  H  I
D  X  E  M  E  W  N  S  I  R  E  V  L  E  N  I  A  U  B  M  W
E  R  R  P  J  E  V  T  Q  D  V  R  E  G  T  C  V  P  E  C  S
N  J  E  S  C  H  Y  R  I  U  J  A  E  R  J  U  I  E  D  Q  S
T  I  R  E  E  H  E  C  L  Z  E  J  T  C  H  F  L  S  D  H  E
N  M  D  Q  P  D  A  R  W  J  A  E  N  I  O  E  R  O  R  H  N
T  N  R  S  R  L  M  X  T  R  I  Q  Z  N  O  V  A  I  S  T  K
I  Y  A  O  B  P  H  Y  G  B  Z  N  D  E  W  N  E  D  V  B  C
U  L  S  O  T  Y  P  H  U  S  F  E  V  E  R  K  I  R  M  J  A
R  I  O  I  S  T  R  U  G  G  L  I  N  G  A  N  X  V  Y  H  L
D  K  A  P  P  R  E  H  E  N  S  I  O  N  S  T  T  K  Z  R  B
S  M  O  R  T  A  L  T  E  R  R  O  R  S  A  X  H  D  A  X  E
```

Answers on page 177

"THE HAUNTED PALACE" PT. 1

Every word listed is contained within the group of letters. Words can be found in a straight line horizontally, vertically, or diagonally. They may be read either forward or backward.

BANNERS

BEFITTING

DOMINION

FABRIC

FLOAT

GENTLE

GLORY

GREENEST

LUMINOUS

LUTE'S

MUSICALLY

OLDEN

PALACE

PALLID

RAMPARTS

REALM

REARED

ROUND

RULER

SERAPH

SITTING

STATE

SWEET

THRONE

WANDERERS

```
T  S  E  N  E  E  R  G  M  D  C  D  V  X  D  P  Y
J  L  I  S  R  Y  V  M  N  L  U  T  E  S  N  P  L
L  F  U  T  R  X  D  U  P  V  M  G  N  P  D  Z  L
O  N  L  O  P  T  O  L  D  E  N  M  L  A  E  R  A
X  C  L  O  H  R  M  X  L  I  R  Y  T  T  P  C  C
R  G  S  R  A  T  I  P  T  M  Z  U  S  A  B  I  I
K  H  O  X  W  T  N  T  R  L  S  B  L  G  O  R  S
M  N  X  X  Z  A  I  D  W  O  U  C  W  E  T  B  U
E  E  W  I  S  F  O  C  M  P  R  M  P  O  R  A  M
F  I  V  A  E  S  N  S  J  S  X  D  I  G  H  F  Y
S  M  C  B  N  C  T  H  P  A  R  E  S  N  L  R  A
T  I  D  X  A  D  A  R  J  V  S  R  L  M  O  Q  B
E  S  T  I  W  N  E  L  A  G  A  A  W  W  Y  U  Z
E  T  U  T  L  X  N  R  A  P  G  E  N  T  L  E  S
W  A  G  P  I  L  I  E  E  P  M  R  J  S  M  J  N
S  T  Z  Y  O  N  A  I  R  R  W  A  Q  Z  R  H  K
C  E  K  D  Q  X  G  P  L  S  S  Q  R  L  I  T  A
```

Answers on page 177

"THE HAUNTED PALACE" PT. 2

Every word listed is contained within the group of letters. Words can be found in a straight line horizontally, vertically, or diagonally. They may be read either forward or backward.

BLOOMED

BLUSHED

DESOLATE

ECHOES

ENTOMBED

FLOWING

FORMS

GHASTLY

GLORY

GLOWING

HIDEOUS

MORROW

PALACE

PALE

PEARL

ROUND

SMILE

SORROW

STORY

SWEET

VALLEY

WINDOWS

WISDOM

```
I  Q  R  O  C  N  E  Z  S  W  O  D  N  I  W  H  T
B  Y  G  I  F  A  X  T  E  S  Q  R  H  S  U  N  K
T  U  G  W  O  S  C  C  J  W  D  Q  F  U  W  T  U
G  E  L  T  C  T  A  R  E  E  M  Q  E  P  P  Y  Z
N  C  E  R  H  L  N  C  B  E  T  V  S  N  A  E  P
I  A  G  W  A  Z  M  M  I  N  T  E  M  L  C  L  R
W  K  N  P  S  N  O  J  G  Y  O  A  I  C  B  L  E
O  D  I  C  G  T  J  H  W  H  R  A  L  Q  R  A  A
L  N  W  A  N  J  A  W  C  L  O  O  E  O  A  V  W
F  U  O  E  F  S  O  E  X  A  A  W  L  M  S  Z  J
R  O  L  N  T  R  Q  L  F  V  C  X  C  G  F  E  H
J  R  G  L  R  K  C  G  Q  O  W  O  R  R  O  S  D
Y  O  Y  O  R  S  U  O  E  D  I  H  J  Y  R  V  I
B  J  M  H  T  S  W  I  S  D  O  M  B  H  M  E  K
S  R  F  O  D  Y  S  D  E  H  S  U  L  B  S  S  E
T  Q  R  Z  Z  T  P  R  O  H  I  P  E  A  R  L  W
V  Y  P  S  W  G  H  K  U  P  D  E  M  O  O  L  B
```

Answers on page 177

"THE CONQUEROR WORM" PT.1

Every word listed is contained within the group of letters. Words can be found in a straight line horizontally, vertically, or diagonally. They may be read either forward or backward.

ANGEL

BEWINGED

BIDDING

CONDOR

DROWNED

FEARS

FLAPPING

FORMLESS

GALA NIGHT

HIGH

HITHER

HOPES

INVISIBLE

LONESOME

MIMES

MUMBLE

ORCHESTRA

PUPPETS

SCENERY

SPHERES

THEATRE

THITHER

```
X  G  G  N  I  P  P  A  L  F  S  G  V  B  F
S  O  R  C  H  E  S  T  R  A  S  J  J  L  P
K  R  B  K  I  P  D  F  O  R  M  L  E  S  S
I  D  A  M  H  U  N  E  C  O  N  D  O  R  T
Z  X  Z  E  S  P  J  U  G  M  Q  Q  P  H  X
I  E  R  E  F  P  H  Y  C  N  E  H  G  X  J
U  E  P  T  Q  E  D  V  R  E  I  I  S  N  U
S  O  V  E  M  T  L  R  L  E  N  W  E  S  P
H  E  S  H  U  S  R  B  O  A  N  G  E  L  R
L  O  N  E  S  O  M  E  L  W  D  E  A  B  E
L  Q  Q  I  O  U  J  A  H  N  N  S  C  Z  H
S  E  M  I  M  O  G  L  G  T  S  E  L  S  T
B  I  D  D  I  N  G  V  V  X  I  P  D  K  I
I  N  V  I  S  I  B  L  E  R  P  H  I  G  H
E  R  T  A  E  H  T  T  Q  M  U  V  T  W  Q
```

Answers on page 178

"THE CONQUEROR WORM" PT. 2

Every word listed is contained within the group of letters. Words can be found in a straight line horizontally, vertically, or diagonally. They may be read either forward or backward.

ANGELS

CIRCLE

CROWD

FOOD

FORGOT

FUNERAL

HORROR

HUMAN

INTRUDE

LIGHTS

MADNESS

MIMIC

MORTAL

MOTLEY DRAMA

PALLID

PHANTOM

PLOT

SEIZE

SIN

SOUL

SPOT

TRAGEDY

UPRISING

VERMIN

WRITHES

```
Y  H  O  B  V  R  T  W  N  B  H  T  X  N  G  A  F
Z  I  C  S  R  D  Y  G  O  S  T  I  Q  X  I  K  L
V  E  X  R  E  F  N  B  E  L  M  O  Y  T  W  L  N
T  S  U  R  O  I  T  K  A  L  V  Q  P  A  A  L  N
J  N  P  R  S  W  Z  B  E  A  C  L  H  S  N  A  E
B  S  G  I  U  F  D  E  N  R  D  R  Q  O  G  T  H
E  O  R  N  L  V  Q  Y  P  E  W  I  I  S  E  R  I
T  P  R  T  Z  K  F  H  H  N  Z  H  L  C  L  O  F
U  X  M  R  L  O  Y  Z  A  U  Y  V  U  L  S  M  P
O  U  H  U  O  M  H  S  N  F  M  S  Q  M  A  K  H
O  M  O  D  A  A  B  E  T  I  F  D  S  W  A  P  H
A  I  R  E  T  D  V  H  O  Z  M  I  K  K  S  N  A
W  M  R  X  O  N  P  T  M  P  T  R  A  G  E  D  Y
Z  I  O  G  L  E  L  I  G  H  T  S  E  R  X  J  F
T  C  R  Q  P  S  K  R  M  L  I  B  F  V  F  Z  A
L  U  O  S  I  S  R  W  H  N  E  W  G  I  U  F  I
M  O  T  L  E  Y  D  R  A  M  A  H  E  E  A  D  L
```

Answers on page 178

"TO ONE IN PARADISE"

Every word listed is contained within the group of letters. Words can be found in a straight line horizontally, vertically, or diagonally. They may be read either forward or backward.

ARISE

BLOOM

BRIGHT

DREAMS

ETERNAL

ETHEREAL

FLOWERS

FOOTSTEP

FOUNTAIN

FRUITS

FUTURE

GLANCES

GREEN ISLE

HOVERING

LANGUAGE

LIGHT

LOVE

MOTIONLESS

OVERCAST

PAST

SHORE

SOLEMN

SOUL

STRICKEN

TRANCES

```
F F F O U N T A I N B H F U Y C H
O L D F H S H H K E A Z A R I S E
O O W L L O H C G W V E C V T O E
T W L B A A V O C I Q O D L H L I
S E L S I N E E R G L M L W K E J
T R X V V N G R R E J Z C M K M C
E S N G Z E E U E I Z F A W D N B
P W P A L U Z K A H N B L O O M G
P G K C G X A C C G T G P J V L X
T M I B R I G H T I E E G O A S L
M O T I O N L E S S R T S N T E A
D S Z H T D K C E T R T C P D W N
F U M F U T U R E A I E S A S F R
N N G A N X M N N S S U W S Y S E
C T R W E J I C W B N H R T Z O T
T X G L W R E X A D H H W F G U E
G T I D F S D T S A C R E V O L M
```

Answers on page 178

"THE CITY IN THE SEA" PT. 1

Every word listed is contained within the group of letters. Words can be found in a straight line horizontally, vertically, or diagonally. They may be read either forward or backward.

ALONE	HEAVEN
BABYLON	SHRINE
BAD	SHRINES
BENEATH	SPIRES
BEST	THRONE
BLEND	TOWERS
DEATH	TOWN
DIM	TURRETS
DOWN	VIOLET
ETERNAL	WATERS
GLEAMS	WINDS
GOOD	WORST

```
K F A T M D O S E N I R H S B G Q
E R F X J O W U P F W N D T L X C
B N D J F D O W N I O Y A H E G T
E Q G T W N E B H S R P X R N I W
N L F Z Y Z N Y R B S E F O D Y D
E S L A H N W O T V T A S N H O D
A E R T Q L A V P B E A H E T V F
T Z A E A M G S A E T E R N A L N
H E T F W K W B S D A B I L J R N
D F E U L O Y K W U E Z N D V V S
D I M N R L T A P A S F E G O O D
U G S F O R Y U O P T H E A V E N
X G L N T L E Z P Y D E G B I E W
X T S E B U A T S Y F C R K O R I
A D B V A T G R S J M W K S L P N
N V R G N M A M T R L B S M E M D
W P B Y J N S P E I D H Y D T A S
```

Answers on page 178

"THE CITY IN THE SEA" PT. 2

Every word listed is contained within the group of letters. Words can be found in a straight line horizontally, vertically, or diagonally. They may be read either forward or backward.

BREATHING

DEAD

DIAMOND

EARTHLY

FANES

FEEBLY

GAPING

HAPPIER

HEAVINGS

HIDEOUSLY

LUMINOUS

MOVEMENT

REDDER

REVERENCE

RICHES

RIPPLES

SETTLE

SINKING

SWELLINGS

THOUSAND

TOWERS

VOID

WATERS

WILDERNESS

YAWN

```
H  Q  Q  B  M  O  V  E  M  E  N  T  Y  E  L  V  X
S  I  H  G  J  J  V  C  L  E  K  K  E  J  S  P  D
S  E  I  N  D  Q  W  U  F  Y  L  B  E  E  F  W  Q
E  C  D  I  N  M  P  I  D  N  A  S  U  O  H  T  D
T  N  E  H  R  I  P  P  L  E  S  S  E  H  C  I  R
T  E  O  T  S  Y  S  R  E  D  D  E  R  R  O  L  D
L  R  U  A  T  R  F  I  L  Y  E  T  O  V  D  I  X
E  E  S  E  J  H  E  A  N  N  X  R  C  B  A  I  T
V  V  L  R  Q  S  E  T  W  K  G  F  N  M  E  R  T
H  E  Y  B  S  W  B  A  A  R  I  M  O  E  D  O  O
A  R  H  A  Y  E  Y  B  V  W  N  N  G  S  S  E  W
P  F  S  P  L  L  V  P  G  I  D  X  G  E  Q  S  E
P  B  Q  M  H  L  E  P  G  B  N  V  K  N  P  Z  R
I  D  H  Y  T  I  G  A  P  I  N  G  I  A  B  W  S
E  L  U  S  R  N  U  L  A  Z  K  J  S  F  R  P  F
R  J  H  Z  A  G  D  S  U  O  N  I  M  U  L  W  F
O  W  H  R  E  S  A  V  X  S  N  U  Q  F  G  J  S
```

Answers on page 179

"SILENCE"

Every word listed is contained within the group of letters. Words can be found in a straight line horizontally, vertically, or diagonally. They may be read either forward or backward.

COMMEND	MEMORIES
CORPORATE	POWER
DOUBLE	QUALITIES
DREAD	REGIONS
DWELLS	SHADOW
ENTITY	SHORE
EVIL	SILENCE
EVINCED	SOLEMN
FOOT	SOLID
GRASS	SOUL
HIMSELF	SPRINGS
INCORPORATE	TEARFUL
LONELY	TERRORLESS
MATTER	URGENT

```
S  A  T  S  I  L  E  N  C  E  S  M  S  I  G  C  I
S  R  S  O  Q  D  C  R  P  O  D  S  W  H  S  I  X
E  I  D  E  O  A  I  T  L  E  A  Z  Q  S  O  U  L
L  N  R  J  N  F  P  E  C  R  M  E  U  L  I  S  S
R  C  E  C  R  T  M  N  G  V  T  T  A  N  K  P  P
O  O  A  P  L  N  I  B  B  E  H  A  L  K  D  E  R
R  R  D  X  R  V  X  T  F  P  I  R  I  C  S  L  I
R  P  O  W  E  R  C  J  Y  D  E  O  T  E  I  O  N
E  O  V  T  G  L  D  W  Q  T  W  P  I  V  D  G  G
T  R  M  N  I  V  N  E  T  T  Z  R  E  R  O  H  S
R  A  Y  E  O  S  E  A  H  M  O  O  S  X  L  B  B
D  T  C  G  N  J  M  I  C  M  Y  C  W  U  S  D  T
W  E  Z  R  S  R  M  Q  E  L  Y  O  F  N  U  H  R
E  E  L  U  H  S  O  M  E  V  D  R  A  V  S  B  C
L  O  N  A  E  F  C  N  J  A  A  K  I  L  B  Z  D
L  C  Z  L  R  T  O  A  H  E  C  D  O  U  B  L  E
S  L  F  D  I  L  O  S  T  X  Y  M  N  N  Y  Z  J
```

Answers on page 179

"DREAM-LAND" PT. 1

Every word listed is contained within the group of letters. Words can be found in a straight line horizontally, vertically, or diagonally. They may be read either forward or backward.

ANGELS

ASPIRE

BOTTOMLESS

BOUNDLESS

CAVES

CHASMS

DISCOVER

DRIP

EIDOLON

EVERMORE

FIRE

HAUNTED

LANDS

LONELY

MOUNTAINS

NIGHT

OBSCURE

OUTSPREAD

REACHED

SHORE

SNOWS

SPACE

SUBLIME

THRONE

TIME

TITAN WOODS

ULTIMATE

UPRIGHT

WATERS

WEIRD CLIME

```
J  L  D  S  T  E  M  I  L  C  D  R  I  E  W  N  Q
C  S  H  O  N  F  N  E  S  I  Y  E  M  I  T  N  K
S  R  B  O  T  T  O  M  L  E  S  S  T  W  I  X  I
T  S  R  M  E  T  A  M  I  T  L  U  X  N  D  Y  W
S  H  E  X  H  Z  E  M  I  L  B  U  S  E  U  B  D
T  N  G  L  E  S  R  E  T  A  W  C  C  L  E  A  V
F  Y  T  I  D  D  P  G  T  N  Q  A  G  M  E  R  H
D  L  A  B  R  N  P  I  R  D  P  V  X  R  N  T  Q
I  E  W  N  G  P  U  T  P  S  G  E  P  O  I  R  N
S  N  I  A  T  N  U  O  M  G  Z  S  L  T  E  V  S
C  O  E  R  I  F  G  F  B  N  T  O  A  A  O  L  O
O  L  V  S  R  W  S  V  E  U  D  N  C  H  E  B  U
V  P  N  N  I  G  H  T  O  I  W  H  J  G  S  H  E
E  E  R  O  M  R  E  V  E  O  E  Q  N  C  V  N  R
R  Q  X  W  W  D  A  C  O  D  F  A  U  N  Z  G  O
V  Q  R  S  R  P  M  D  R  Q  P  R  P  N  F  I  H
L  Y  G  I  P  A  S  P  I  R  E  C  H  A  S  M  S
```

Answers on page 179

"DREAM-LAND" PT. 2

Every word listed is contained within the group of letters. Words can be found in a straight line horizontally, vertically, or diagonally. They may be read either forward or backward.

AGONY	HEAVEN	SHROUDED
CHILLY	LAKES	SNOWS
DEAD	LONE	START
DISMAL	MELANCHOLY	SWAMP
DWELL	MOUNTAINS	TOAD
EARTH	MURMURING	TRAVELLER
ENCAMP	PASS	UNHOLY
FRIENDS	PAST	WANDERER
GHOULS	SHEETED	WHITE-ROBED

```
J  N  R  P  P  K  H  D  E  N  O  L  Y  L  Z  D  G
T  Q  N  E  D  M  S  V  W  F  N  M  G  L  D  P  Q
X  Y  U  U  R  H  U  T  X  Q  L  A  K  E  S  M  Y
G  F  V  Q  N  E  L  R  R  J  J  L  I  Z  Z  A  Q
W  Z  R  W  O  Y  D  P  M  A  W  S  L  I  S  C  P
N  L  L  O  H  M  L  N  G  U  T  A  Y  E  K  N  O
E  S  W  O  N  S  O  O  A  P  R  S  P  Q  W  E  H
V  H  O  S  O  T  N  U  H  W  A  I  M  K  H  D  Y
A  X  M  C  S  Y  F  Y  N  N  N  A  N  O  I  Q  L
E  A  H  A  G  A  H  Q  D  T  U  S  R  G  T  D  L
H  Q  P  J  N  T  P  T  A  L  A  D  K  M  E  E  I
L  F  X  Z  R  O  E  G  E  Y  A  I  O  Y  R  T  H
K  M  K  A  N  A  F  H  D  I  J  M  N  U  O  E  C
W  N  E  Q  F  D  E  D  U  O  R  H  S  S  B  E  F
C  Q  Y  L  O  H  C  N  A  L  E  M  S  I  E  H  N
S  D  N  E  I  R  F  G  H  O  U  L  S  Z  D  S  W
T  R  A  V  E  L  L  E  R  G  U  M  V  O  Y  N  Y
```

Answers on page 179

"DREAM-LAND" PT. 3

Every word listed is contained within the group of letters. Words can be found in a straight line horizontally, vertically, or diagonally. They may be read either forward or backward. Leftover letters will reveal an interesting bit of trivia about Poe's legend.

DARE	LEGION	SOUL
DARKENED	LONELY	SPIRIT
ELDORADO	MYSTERIES	TRAVELLING
EXPOSED	NIGHT	ULTIMATE
FORBID	OBSCURE	UNCLOSED
FRINGED	OPENLY	UPLIFTING
HAUNTED	PASSES	UPRIGHT
HEART	PEACEFUL	WANDERED
HUMAN	REGION	
KING	SHADOW	

```
E  L  D  O  R  A  D  O  T  D  S  O  U  L  U
G  W  A  N  D  E  R  E  D  H  P  R  E  P  H
N  U  N  C  L  O  S  E  D  E  G  G  R  E  Y
I  S  E  D  E  T  N  U  A  H  I  I  A  L  S
K  T  H  U  M  A  N  C  A  O  G  R  N  D  P
M  R  P  A  S  S  E  S  N  H  T  E  L  I  I
A  A  E  N  D  F  D  W  T  A  P  S  1  B  R
D  V  X  S  U  O  T  P  U  O  B  L  I  R  I
E  E  P  L  S  H  W  R  E  G  I  O  N  O  T
N  L  O  E  S  E  I  R  E  T  S  Y  M  F  D
E  L  S  I  N  1  G  N  I  T  F  I  L  P  U
K  I  E  R  U  C  S  B  O  8  4  E  4  I  N
R  N  D  Y  L  E  N  O  L  G  R  R  A  H  A
A  G  F  R  I  N  G  E  D  M  S  A  M  A  G
D  A  Z  E  T  A  M  I  T  L  U  D  I  N  E
```

Hidden Message: _____

_____

"A DREAM WITHIN A DREAM"

Every word listed is contained within the group of letters. Words can be found in a straight line horizontally, vertically, or diagonally. They may be read either forward or backward.

AVOW	KISS
BROW	NIGHT
CLASP	PARTING
CREEP	PITILESS
DAYS	ROAR
DEEM	SEEM
DREAM	SHORE
FINGERS	STAND
FLOWN	THEREFORE
GOLDEN SAND	VISION
GONE	WEEP
GRASP	WITHIN
HAND	WRONG
HOPE	

```
C K W S W I Z N P P X S P A G E H
X G M U S G N O R W B S S T B V B
S B Q F A E V U W Z D E A C P U V
W W Q M C H L Y U Q C N L U R J F
W E E X X S Y I S S A O C V G Y S
L E U H F P A R T I N G F X N S H
S P G B M G A Y W I G A P I I C G
Z G S Q R V R Y V R P E G K G R A
D O L R H O S P A N W R E R H E F
L L E O E V A S Q K N R L N T E M
G D P R W G P R Y F O M W Q E P W
D E D S O A N P U F E O V P Z K I
D N N O R H W I E M L I G O M C T
P S A T B O S R F F S G B B A D H
H A T H V D E K T I G Y E U E Q I
F N S A P H T J O C R M A E R L N
K D R B T M E N N C R Z M D D W O
```

Answers on page 180

"THE TELL-TALE HEART" PT. 1

Every word listed is contained within the group of letters. Words can be found in a straight line horizontally, vertically, or diagonally. They may be read either forward or backward.

ABOVE

CALMLY

DESTROYED

DISEASE

DREADFULLY

DULLED

EARTH

HEALTHILY

HEARING

HEARKEN

HEAVEN

HELL

MAD

NERVOUS

OBSERVE

SENSES

SHARPENED

THINGS

WHOLE

```
D U L L E D D D E Y O R T S E D N
H C M Y N A D R W H O L E M T Q O
E S D D M U I Y T I T A Y V B E L
A H I K R O S N S C F R Y M O V U
V A T G V Q E Y W M A U A J H R I
E R A D R E A D F U L L Y E S E Z
N P F G L S S R U X W V A U N S K
Q E S C T P E R J X A L O E S B K
W N D S Z T A S Y R T V K P A O J
P E U V N P X T N H R R I B R F H
I D F W C M Z F I E A E O N X E O
N L K K A A C L N E S V T A E K
L L E H J E Y O H E E I H R S W E
Y V L V C C A L M L Y H I A P G N
C M G Z U G T L F P V N N F X D Q
Y Y J X J F T B J L G R G J E G Q
L X G N V C E B C T V O S T N K A
```

Answers on page 180

"THE TELL-TALE HEART" PT. 2

Every word listed is contained within the group of letters. Words can be found in a straight line horizontally, vertically, or diagonally. They may be read either forward or backward.

BLOOD	LIFE
BRAIN	LOVED
COLD	MIND
DAY	MYSELF
DESIRE	NIGHT
ENTERED	NONE
EYE	OLD MAN
FILM	ONCE
FIRST	PASSION
GIVEN	TAKE
GOLD	THINK
HAUNTED	VULTURE
INSULT	

```
T N V O X C T Q J O H H Y P S J U
G G Y C A Y V A D N F V O J E S B
W A D V B O B Z D C A I L T G B V
D B M A P N L J G E R I L I R I D
U A Z V D V O J F V F L E M B N N
F L E S Y M O O V E N O N I H E I
Z S Q I U B D N V R F Q L A A V M
W X M T T E T I H F Z N Z F U I X
D E Z C D R H A X A A A W L N G E
Y E W A Y I G R G M J D T G T J T
U S V C U S I B D H L U L S E U T
V X J O T E N L L O R S Z J D S C
X S C O L D O Z G E P T G A R Z T
I I N S U L T A Y H Y K Y I B H G
A L H H D B G E Q D E V F Z I W T
N Q W H V P S P A S S I O N J N S
R F E N T E R E D Y T A K E P X L
```

Answers on page 180

Every word listed is contained within the group of letters. Words can be found in a straight line horizontally, vertically, or diagonally. They may be read either forward or backward.

BED	KINDER
BOLDLY	LATCH
BROKE	LAUGHED
CALLING	MADMEN
CAUTION	MIDNIGHT
CHAMBER	OPENED
CLOSED	ROOM
CREAKED	SHONE
DISTURB	SINGLE
EVIL EYE	SUSPECT
HEAD	VEXED
INQUIRING	WISELY

```
V R S P P D P K N S D M N E P Z E
U S U D M V E X E D S E O S T N C
C M N L A T C H A I E X O O O D N
Y L D L O B U E N S K K J H R V R
O A M D G Z H G Z T S E S P U U C
D E H G U A L A P U F V G D E B I
L M A F S E R Q F R Y N M E G R Q
G T C E P S U S S B I A T Y N O C
N O I T U A C C Z R D T C E I K B
V H T H G I N D I M K R N L L E X
L A W C W K P U E Y E M I I L B Z
A C I L C I Q N N A L K V V A M Z
H J V O B N W C K L R E W E C H B
J E E S I D R E G G Z S S Q G P W
B O P E N E D T A L D F X I Y M J
F Y H D I R N H B O V M Y C W U T
L G C H A M B E R H U T Y U M K L
```

Answers on page 181

"THE TELL-TALE HEART" PT. 4

Every word listed is contained within the group of letters. Words can be found in a straight line horizontally, vertically, or diagonally. They may be read either forward or backward.

BACK	PITCH
BLACK	POWERS
DARKNESS	PUSHING
DOOR	QUICKLY
DREAM	ROBBERS
EIGHTH	SCARCELY
EXTENT	STARTLED
HEARD	STEADILY
MINUTE	SUDDENLY
MOVED	THOUGHTS
MOVES	TRIUMPH
NIGHT	UPON
OPENING	

```
G G G T A W R K F D P U T S C S H
Y R L D O G O B S E D Z X P Z J F
Q N P K J L B I E L O X E T D T D
K D O X K Y B C V T M A M X S R Y
D C T P B H E M O R Y O B F T I L
R R A D U H R H M A D Z H H E U K
G O A L V T S B P T Y C G G A M C
V Q O E B H A A X S T I N N D P I
V K P D H G W C Q I N M I I I H U
B T G A U I R K P Y T A H N L W Q
S C A R C E L Y I H L E S E Y X Z
S N Y K K S K I O C R R U P X R D
E U I N M I N U T E M D P O X S T
E X T E N T G R I P O W E R S L P
W O M S P H W M U O V I F K O Y E
L K G S T T T D W P E E N W B O I
V O P S A I S L S U D D E N L Y N
```

Answers on page 181

"THE TELL-TALE HEART" PT. 5

Every word listed is contained within the group of letters. Words can be found in a straight line horizontally, vertically, or diagonally. They may be read either forward or backward.

BED

CRYING

DOWN

FASTENING

HEAD

HEAR

HEARKENING

KEPT

LANTERN

LISTENING

MOVE

MUSCLE

NIGHT

OLD

OPEN

SPRANG

STILL

THUMB

TIME

UPON

WALL

WATCHES

WHOLE HOUR

```
H E A R K E N I N G S G W E H L O
M U S C L E V H P A N F T I U P E
W Z V G E Y P J G I R L Z Q I V L
X Z E X G F F U N C W L C F O P J
O B T E M I T E L H V A R R Y O R
T W E K H L T A O V H E U M A C I
P N U D K S N L S P R A N G R Q G
E K E U A T E U U C B E I H O L N
K S X F E H G M P E R U A X A M I
S T H R O D B Q O O Y Z M S S Q N
Y I N U E Q I U B V N M N E F U E
B L R G S N I L L S E D H E C M T
H L K F D T S Q B I O C L R P L S
X U L A I H N I G H T H Y O H O I
C R E A G U N E I A A I E C O S L
S H Q W W M D O W N N E I A X G H
E O H J C B J R U G Z E B Z R F N
```

Answers on page 181

Every word listed is contained within the group of letters. Words can be found in a straight line horizontally, vertically, or diagonally. They may be read either forward or backward.

ARISES	MERELY
BOSOM	MORTAL
BOTTOM	MOUSE
CHIMNEY	PAIN
COMFORT	PITIED
DEATH	ROOM
DREADFUL	SHADOW
FEARS	SLIGHT
GRIEF	SOUND
GROAN	TERRORS
GROWING	WELLED
HEART	WORLD

```
A M I N Y W M A D B L V D E G V W
V V S M G O O Q T C X T V S K J D
L Q O F O F U R B Y Q R H U T L B
Y I U R E R N B L V A A M O E O O
F Q N X S A O R L D D E Y M R K T
F U D H L S R Y T O R H E G R W T
K Y U O O A Y S W E D I N N O U O
R D L M D R F X L E L H M D R S M
E J A H E P Y Y L B A U I E S G Y
V J C Y A T K L O O T G H I U N B
X U Q S T M E L C V R Y C T E I T
N H D E H W L D O R O K D I F W H
A V X S T K T R O F M O C P G O G
O G V I P A K X Y U Y Q D T H R I
R V Y R A K H J J Y L F E I R G L
G T Z A I K M H D R E A D F U L S
C S A M N E M R V K W V W P G B G
```

Every word listed is contained within the group of letters. Words can be found in a straight line horizontally, vertically, or diagonally. They may be read either forward or backward.

BONES	LENGTH
CHILLED	LITTLE
DIRECTED	MARROW
DOWN	OPENED
FURIOUS	PERFECT
GAZED	PERSON
HEARING	SINGLE
HIDEOUS	SPIDER
IMAGINE	THREAD
INSTINCT	WAITED
LANTERN	WIDE

```
S  S  M  H  R  Y  D  K  O  H  C  M  T  T  R  Y  Z
E  O  W  B  T  F  K  J  I  M  B  L  C  B  K  I  J
N  A  R  U  U  G  U  O  J  D  N  E  N  E  P  O
O  P  O  H  T  D  N  A  G  R  Q  P  F  O  P  C  I
B  D  S  H  J  C  F  E  E  G  V  O  R  M  W  N  F
W  A  I  T  E  D  B  T  L  T  Q  X  E  F  S  U  U
D  X  R  W  S  E  N  I  G  A  M  I  P  T  H  L  R
E  I  U  Z  P  A  U  W  Y  G  N  W  I  R  I  W  I
Z  A  R  H  L  X  C  P  O  Z  Y  N  B  T  C  G  O
A  J  G  E  I  W  Z  Z  R  A  C  L  T  S  H  X  U
G  L  F  A  C  D  O  B  E  T  Z  L  A  P  I  A  S
N  G  Y  R  G  T  E  R  L  L  E  S  B  I  L  Z  D
W  R  I  I  Y  D  E  O  R  W  G  B  G  D  L  A  T
O  I  U  N  I  B  J  D  U  A  P  N  V  E  E  X  Y
D  Z  D  G  R  I  H  D  B  S  M  F  I  R  D  O  H
I  N  P  E  E  A  Y  Q  C  S  S  Y  H  S  R  P  E
U  P  E  R  S  O  N  V  S  F  B  T  B  W  I  W  X
```

Answers on page 182

Every word listed is contained within the group of letters. Words can be found in a straight line horizontally, vertically, or diagonally. They may be read either forward or backward.

ACUTENESS	LOW
BEATING	MADNESS
BEATING	MISTAKE
CAME	OLD
COTTON	QUICK SOUND
COURAGE	SENSES
EARS	SOLDIER
ENVELOPED	SOUND
FURY	STIMULATES
HEART	TOLD
INCREASED	WATCH
KNEW	

```
A V B S F P J V G V F S D P U O W
Q X E U I G N I T A E B E N J S O
X V R A K T O S N U H D K S U K L
I Y P T R A E H S T G Z Q F N O A
G J A N Z S E H O R N G U E I E S
I P F A S N R L E V S A W N Y G S
M U F S O D D C P L C K C O R S S
R Q V Z S U A K O T G R U H D E S
S C F N U E V L U U E O C P E T E
O P A G O O N Q Y A R T V J P A N
L W V M I T X E S V A A U S O L D
D T J M E C T E T W M O G Z L U A
I X N O E N D O O U F W Q E E M M
E K H U L Z Q B C Y C H B G V I X
R N H W T D B M I S T A K E N T D
H X Q U I C K S O U N D C E E S R
N H P K X W B C G Q X J Q X K P N
```

Answers on page 182

"THE TELL-TALE HEART" PT. 9

Every word listed is contained within the group of letters. Words can be found in a straight line horizontally, vertically, or diagonally. They may be read either forward or backward.

BEATING

BURST

CEASED

CORPSE

DEED

DRAGGED

DREADFUL

EXAMINED

EXTREME

HEART

HELLISH

LANTERN

LEAPED

LOUD YELL

LOUDER

MINUTES

MUFFLED

NEIGHBOR

NERVOUS

PULSATION

QUICKER

REFRAINED

SCARCELY

SHRIEKED

UNCONTROLLABLE

```
X  Z  U  H  B  L  Y  D  E  K  E  I  R  H  S  R  C
V  T  L  U  E  E  X  A  M  I  N  E  D  T  Y  Z  S
N  E  R  C  G  L  C  K  R  A  F  E  A  X  O  P  C
E  S  P  R  O  C  L  Z  K  R  S  L  A  H  L  G  Y
T  M  B  E  X  E  F  I  A  C  A  Q  J  J  Z  I  L
L  E  P  Y  A  C  Q  I  S  N  E  R  V  O  U  S  E
O  L  P  P  E  U  N  L  T  H  M  H  P  W  N  D  C
D  V  E  A  I  E  L  E  A  I  U  C  U  B  E  R  R
X  D  S  C  D  E  R  T  N  N  F  L  A  E  I  E  A
F  E  K  S  Y  N  D  U  S  H  F  O  D  A  G  A  C
D  E  F  D  Q  R  T  I  E  E  L  U  E  T  H  D  S
R  U  U  O  A  E  Y  R  K  A  E  D  M  I  B  F  A
H  O  M  G  S  C  S  E  H  R  D  E  B  N  O  U  N
L  P  G  G  N  A  E  W  P  T  Q  R  X  G  R  L  J
L  E  U  N  O  I  T  A  S  L  U  P  Z  T  F  L  V
D  E  L  B  A  L  L  O  R  T  N  O  C  N  U  R  G
B  C  O  V  U  E  M  E  R  T  X  E  W  P  Z  P  N
```

Answers on page 182

"THE TELL-TALE HEART" PT. 10

Every word listed is contained within the group of letters. Words can be found in a straight line horizontally, vertically, or diagonally. They may be read either forward or backward.

ARMS

BLOOD-SPOT

BODY

CAUGHT

CHAMBER

CLEVERLY

CORPSE

CUNNINGLY

DESCRIBE

DETECTED

DISMEMBERED

HASTILY

HEAD

LEGS

LONGER

MAD

PLANKS

PRECAUTIONS

SCANTLINGS

SILENCE

STAIN

THINK

WANED

WASH OUT

WRONG

```
K P C L E V E R L Y S H A S Z C A
J F T H A S T I L Y G Y T D G A R
W T U R L S B A S V N A K J E U M
U R H S I L E N C E I C W D B G S
Z S E I F H G C O N L O Q G I H D
T C G N Z B D W C T R K Z R T E
T U N E K A O M D N P K Z C D N
T N I R L O Y X A L A S U H S I A
O N G A Z A L E G C C E A H E S W
P I N X G R H G Y V S M S K D M N
S N O K P G K I B K B F P E R E U
D G R A D P B S L E S H T M X M M
O L W I X R X Y R E Q E Q E M B X
O Y W Y P L A N K S C Q T A D E N
L J U P R E C A U T I O N S R R M
B Y D O B T E H E K W Z V I T E A
W A S H O U T D N R K G G G Y D D
```

91

Answers on page 182

"THE TELL-TALE HEART" PT. 11

Every word listed is contained within the group of letters. Words can be found in a straight line horizontally, vertically, or diagonally. They may be read either forward or backward.

AROUSED	MADE
DARK	MIDNIGHT
DEPUTED	NEIGHBOR
END	OFFICE
ENTERED	OFFICERS
FEAR	OPEN
HEARD	PERFECT
HOUR	POLICE
INTRODUCED	PREMISES
KNOCKING	SOUNDED
LABORS	STREET
LIGHT	SUSPICION
LODGED	

```
T  J  T  Y  B  L  M  S  Y  E  C  I  F  F  O  R  S
K  R  F  V  Z  Y  K  S  B  P  F  E  C  I  L  O  P
L  A  B  O  R  S  E  N  O  I  C  I  P  S  U  S  D
N  C  N  A  T  S  M  X  G  M  K  T  U  N  R  E  E
Y  Y  N  U  I  H  V  N  Z  X  R  A  D  E  N  S  C
R  L  K  M  O  H  I  D  M  L  Z  E  C  D  Z  O  U
A  G  E  X  H  K  G  A  O  E  D  I  B  I  R  D  D
S  R  T  Q  C  R  Q  R  N  S  F  Z  A  E  M  W  O
P  B  O  O  J  I  R  K  N  F  H  R  O  I  D  O  R
D  Y  N  U  O  T  A  P  O  D  O  R  D  M  E  V  T
E  K  J  P  S  K  E  W  J  B  A  N  I  B  T  C  N
R  Y  E  H  I  E  F  E  H  X  I  R  E  P  U  U  I
E  N  C  U  E  P  D  G  R  G  J  I  R  O  P  Q  L
T  K  R  D  Z  A  I  I  H  T  C  E  F  R  E  P  I
N  V  T  P  Y  E  R  T  Z  Z  S  D  Z  O  D  S  G
E  R  F  L  N  N  E  D  X  Q  O  E  J  R  U  O  H
E  D  F  J  M  V  H  L  O  D  G  E  D  A  M  F  T
```

Answers on page 183

"THE TELL-TALE HEART" PT. 12

Every word listed is contained within the group of letters. Words can be found in a straight line horizontally, vertically, or diagonally. They may be read either forward or backward.

ABSENT

AUDACITY

BADE

CHAIRS

CHAMBER

CORPSE

COUNTRY

DESIRED

FATIGUES

HOUSE

LENGTH

MENTIONED

MYSELF

OVER

REST

SEARCH

SHRIEK

SMILED

TREASURES

TRIUMPH

WELCOME

```
S  E  U  G  I  T  A  F  H  B  W  O  I  P  V  E  B
L  H  C  R  A  E  S  B  K  F  F  L  E  S  Y  M  X
Y  E  V  R  S  U  B  U  I  I  T  J  J  W  P  O  G
M  E  N  T  I  O  N  E  D  F  C  N  N  T  U  C  V
W  G  W  G  D  W  E  Q  T  E  Q  H  I  I  Y  L  F
R  B  Y  R  T  N  U  O  C  R  R  N  A  Q  E  E  P
Q  A  D  W  C  H  V  O  T  S  I  I  B  M  M  W  Y
P  U  A  U  L  X  V  K  H  S  E  U  S  T  B  X  X
L  D  B  A  K  E  A  R  R  U  E  M  E  N  E  C
P  A  S  Q  R  Q  I  E  Y  U  W  R  Q  P  D  P  R
G  C  E  P  S  E  R  U  S  A  E  R  T  R  H  L  E
A  I  N  B  K  H  J  L  M  B  L  P  T  X  O  M  E
P  T  T  W  X  L  P  P  I  Q  B  B  V  D  U  A  F
E  Y  C  H  A  I  R  S  L  Y  Z  I  Q  S  S  M  J
D  E  Q  L  H  D  A  M  E  K  G  V  J  D  E  I  C
A  C  S  H  W  Y  J  T  D  T  M  C  O  R  P  S  E
B  D  O  X  Q  P  H  L  X  N  E  V  I  B  R  K  E
```

Answers on page 183

Every word listed is contained within the group of letters. Words can be found in a straight line horizontally, vertically, or diagonally. They may be read either forward or backward.

ACHED	GONE
CHATTED	LENGTH
CHEERILY	LONG
DISTINCT	MANNER
EARS	NOISE
EASE	OFFICERS
FAMILIAR	PALE
FANCIED	RINGING
FEELING	SATISFIED
FREELY	WISHED
GAINED	

```
W  G  N  O  L  L  I  Z  M  C  X  X  R  P  H  V  G
S  A  T  I  S  F  I  E  D  Q  D  O  U  E  V  S  O
E  N  O  G  Z  X  Y  L  E  F  I  E  L  K  L  N  F
N  W  X  H  A  O  B  D  H  E  R  F  N  E  P  G  F
Q  D  T  Z  G  Q  C  O  C  F  E  E  L  I  N  G  I
I  Y  C  O  X  H  N  A  A  J  M  E  E  D  A  D  C
D  Q  N  L  A  G  L  C  H  E  E  R  I  L  Y  G  E
J  P  I  T  F  A  N  C  I  E  D  N  P  M  Y  K  R
G  P  T  K  H  D  T  X  M  M  G  A  J  O  Q  O  S
G  E  S  T  D  F  D  N  Z  X  L  N  R  U  H  H  R
D  R  I  N  J  D  W  W  G  E  U  D  I  Q  T  A  Z
N  X  D  P  X  H  F  I  B  P  S  M  U  G  I  X  U
W  F  A  D  I  G  T  S  E  S  I  O  N  L  N  E  X
X  F  F  V  M  F  K  H  T  H  Q  E  I  L  C  I  U
F  S  L  Q  D  L  W  E  R  A  L  M  A  N  N  E  R
E  S  A  E  V  A  S  D  D  Y  A  M  M  E  A  R  S
J  V  H  I  T  A  U  J  O  F  Z  S  G  D  X  G  S
```

Answers on page 183

Every word listed is contained within the group of letters. Words can be found in a straight line horizontally, vertically, or diagonally. They may be read either forward or backward. Leftover letters will reveal an interesting bit of trivia about Poe's legend.

ADMIT	LOUDER
AGONY	LOW
ARGUED	OFFICERS
BEATING	SCREAM
CHATTED	SOUND
COTTON	STEADILY
DOUBT	SWUNG
FLOOR	TRIFLES
FLUENTLY	VILLAINS
FOAMED	VIOLENT
GRATED	VOICE
HARK	WATCH

```
T H T E T A D M I T M E L L T A W
L E B H E A R T W A R E D U O L O
C A U S F F L U E N T L Y I R A L
H S O T P U B R L I S H E D G I N
A J D Y A N C U A R Y O F O 1 S 8
T 4 B L 3 S I N T H O E N S O H R
T O E I R T L I V F W Y E U D O T
E B A D O S T O F C A N N M O A N
D G T A D A Z I O I T D N L S E E
N A I E M E C T E D C T F H E E L
P I N T O E T N E E H R P O L E O
W A G S R O S A M A S O S T F L I
K I K S N E L Y R P A W I D I O V
N R L Y T E N G D G O L U L R A R
S F A O R T U H E C I O V N T E G
O T H H I E D E M A O F C F G I C
T I O N D T A L E S N I A L L I V
```

Hidden Message: _____

_____

Answers on page 183

"THE BLACK CAT" PT. 1

Every word listed is contained within the group of letters. Words can be found in a straight line horizontally, vertically, or diagonally. They may be read either forward or backward.

DESTROYED

DREAM

EFFECTS

EVIDENCE

EXPECT

HORROR

HOUSEHOLD

IMMEDIATE

INTELLECT

LOGICAL

NARRATIVE

PEN

PERCEIVE

PHANTASM

SENSES

SOLICIT

SUCCINCTLY

TERRIBLE

TERRIFIED

TORTURED

WILD

WORLD

```
S  U  C  C  I  N  C  T  L  Y  E  H  D  T  U  J  E
C  J  Y  U  U  H  S  B  J  L  Q  X  L  Z  Z  K  V
F  E  D  L  O  H  E  S  U  O  H  Q  I  L  J  N  I
V  T  M  T  U  T  N  O  J  L  J  T  W  N  N  S  E
P  A  S  E  I  T  S  E  V  I  D  E  N  C  E  D  C
T  I  A  D  N  M  E  U  W  R  P  R  E  C  F  M  R
E  D  T  P  T  Q  S  M  E  T  W  R  V  V  F  S  E
R  E  N  W  E  Z  X  A  F  J  T  I  I  K  E  O  P
R  M  A  O  L  K  M  U  K  X  R  B  T  T  C  L  H
I  M  H  R  L  L  A  C  I  G  O  L  A  O  T  I  I
F  I  P  L  E  J  S  P  I  M  R  E  R  R  S  C  J
I  R  A  D  C  O  I  J  T  N  R  X  R  T  X  I  H
E  A  A  P  T  A  Z  S  C  E  O  E  A  U  R  T  K
D  D  E  Y  O  R  T  S  E  D  H  S  N  R  Q  R  L
A  Y  C  W  G  T  R  A  P  L  Y  P  P  E  P  F  Y
O  W  J  A  J  N  A  R  X  Y  G  G  Q  D  I  E  X
H  X  L  H  P  U  R  E  E  G  A  V  K  A  H  I  N
```

Answers on page 184

"THE BLACK CAT" PT. 2

Every word listed is contained within the group of letters. Words can be found in a straight line horizontally, vertically, or diagonally. They may be read either forward or backward.

ANIMALS

BRUTE

CARESSING

CHARACTER

CHERISHED

COMPANIONS

CONSPICUOUS

DERIVED

DIRECTLY

DISPOSITION

DOCILITY

FEEDING

FIDELITY

GROWTH

HUMANITY

INDULGED

INFANCY

INTENSITY

MANHOOD

PALTRY

PARENTS

PECULIARITY

PLEASURE

SAGACIOUS

TENDERNESS

TROUBLE

UNSELFISH

```
Z  S  Y  B  E  O  C  J  R  E  T  C  A  R  A  H  C
L  N  T  C  A  R  E  S  S  I  N  G  X  D  G  U  A
U  O  I  P  Y  T  I  L  I  C  O  D  K  F  P  I  L
L  I  R  E  R  U  S  A  E  L  P  Y  E  U  A  X  V
D  N  A  V  C  R  C  D  E  H  S  I  R  E  H  C  P
I  A  I  U  O  F  E  E  D  I  N  G  S  U  P  A  S
R  P  L  I  N  D  U  L  G  E  D  P  N  B  R  P  S
E  M  U  P  S  H  T  W  O  R  G  S  G  E  R  M  E
C  O  C  A  P  Y  T  I  S  N  E  T  N  I  I  P  N
T  C  E  L  I  F  I  D  E  L  I  T  Y  H  T  K  R
L  M  P  T  C  Y  H  T  F  Q  S  C  L  J  R  K  E
Y  B  P  R  U  I  O  I  J  A  M  A  N  H  O  O  D
B  C  G  Y  O  F  S  L  A  M  I  N  A  O  U  B  N
M  E  D  O  U  H  Z  I  N  F  A  N  C  Y  B  R  E
R  J  H  A  S  A  G  A  C  I  O  U  S  R  L  U  T
B  N  O  I  T  I  S  O  P  S  I  D  G  G  E  T  A
D  E  R  I  V  E  D  H  U  M  A  N  I  T  Y  E  E
```

Answers on page 184

"THE BLACK CAT" PT. 3

Every word listed is contained within the group of letters. Words can be found in a straight line horizontally, vertically, or diagonally. They may be read either forward or backward.

ANCIENT

ANIMAL

BIRDS

BLACK

CAT

DOG

DOMESTIC

FREQUENT

HAPPENS

HEART

HOUSE

INTELLIGENCE

LARGE

MARRIED

MENTION

MONKEY

NAME

NOTION

PLAYMATE

PLUTO

PREVENT

PROCURING

SERIOUS

STREETS

TINCTURED

UNCONGENIAL

WIFE

```
W  K  R  U  Z  A  I  G  P  S  J  E  O  C  I  J  D
Z  W  K  J  K  N  A  F  T  T  S  L  S  N  P  L  A
H  O  S  N  D  E  R  Y  I  E  H  E  W  P  A  V  P
M  R  T  E  R  E  R  A  R  E  N  C  P  I  G  M  R
V  H  X  D  Q  B  N  I  A  R  V  N  N  A  F  D  E
P  I  K  U  V  C  O  R  B  T  B  E  X  N  S  Y  V
Z  G  E  R  I  U  T  A  A  S  G  G  P  I  N  U  E
Z  N  N  E  S  J  D  C  M  N  B  I  L  M  E  O  N
T  D  N  I  Q  E  S  U  O  H  F  L  A  A  P  F  T
I  T  M  W  R  Z  Z  C  V  S  Q  L  Y  L  P  M  M
N  N  F  A  A  U  N  S  D  W  T  E  M  M  A  O  E
C  D  O  G  R  U  C  R  E  E  O  T  A  A  H  N  N
T  P  B  I  A  R  I  O  L  H  W  N  T  N  R  K  T
U  L  L  O  T  B  I  Q  R  A  C  I  E  M  B  E  I
R  U  A  A  J  O  R  E  B  P  R  T  F  O  R  Y  O
E  T  C  L  A  X  N  G  D  E  P  G  I  E  E  D  N
D  O  K  C  I  T  S  E  M  O  D  O  E  W  F  Z  K
```

Answers on page 184

"THE BLACK CAT" PT. 4

Every word listed is contained within the group of letters. Words can be found in a straight line horizontally, vertically, or diagonally. They may be read either forward or backward.

AFFECTION

ALCOHOL

BLUSH

DISEASE

DISPOSITION

EFFECTS

FIEND

FRIENDSHIP

IRRITABLE

MALTREATING

MOODY

PEEVISH

PLUTO

RADICAL

REGARD

REGARDLESS

RESTRAIN

SEVERAL

SUFFERED

TEMPER

TEMPERAMENT

VIOLENCE

WORSE

```
Q M X A E E I H L D I S E A S E V
D I S P O S I T I O N F J C J I F
H S U L B Q R S P T K D O I O H E
S U N H B N P Q I U N N A L H L G
B F U Y L O H O C L A D E F B N J
N F I E N D Y B S P X N R A I P H
O E M O O D Y N L Z C I T T N W B
I R S S V Q L R M E E I A O E R E
T E F F E C T S O N R E N M T C A
C D R E G A R D D R R A J J F D R
E L A R E V E S I T Z H J S W A E
F E S R O W H R L V V Q P K D H S
F R F I Y I K A E P E E V I S H T
A H U T P W M S G P K A C T T D R
R E G A R D L E S S M A B G S D A
D M C Q B W J O B B L E B N V E I
I E T N E M A R E P M E T W M A N
```

Answers on page 184

"THE BLACK CAT" PT. 5

Every word listed is contained within the group of letters. Words can be found in a straight line horizontally, vertically, or diagonally. They may be read either forward or backward.

ATROCITY

AVOIDED

DEBAUCH

DEMON

DROWNED

EYES

FANCIED

FLIGHT

FRAME

FRIGHT

GRASPED

GUILTY

HAUNTS

INFLICTED

INTOXICATED

MALEVOLENCE

ONE NIGHT

ORIGINAL

PEN-KNIFE

PLUNGED

POOR BEAST

REASON

REMORSE

SOCKET

THROAT

WOUND

```
P  T  D  V  F  R  H  P  L  P  Q  I  E  T  V  M  M
D  I  N  F  H  S  T  N  U  A  H  L  H  G  E  G  D
H  E  D  E  I  C  N  A  F  X  N  G  H  W  L  E  D
W  C  N  P  V  G  P  T  V  T  I  I  L  E  T  O  C
Y  E  U  W  N  W  R  Y  S  R  H  E  G  C  W  A  F
M  P  M  A  O  R  P  A  F  A  D  G  I  I  M  L  D
W  R  A  L  B  R  E  L  S  Q  E  L  I  J  R  W  Y
I  N  L  G  R  E  D  A  U  P  F  B  T  N  U  O  T
Y  S  E  L  W  L  D  G  S  N  E  C  R  Z  E  U  I
Y  A  V  O  I  D  E  D  I  O  G  D  R  O  M  N  C
T  A  O  V  E  M  A  R  F  E  N  E  T  O  O  D  O
H  F  L  Q  M  U  P  F  S  Z  S  H  D  Z  J  P  R
R  C  E  F  I  N  K  N  E  P  G  R  V  N  H  Q  T
O  O  N  A  F  M  X  F  R  I  D  E  O  O  X  I  A
A  N  C  U  N  G  U  I  L  T  Y  Y  Q  M  B  S  H
T  T  E  K  C  O  S  F  R  L  K  E  N  E  E  P  X
I  N  T  O  X  I  C  A  T  E  D  S  F  D  K  R  I
```

Answers on page 185

"THE BLACK CAT" PT. 6

Every word listed is contained within the group of letters. Words can be found in a straight line horizontally, vertically, or diagonally. They may be read either forward or backward.

BRUTE

CREATURE

EVIDENT

FRIGHTFUL

HUNG

INFINITE

JUDGMENT

LAW

LOVED

NOOSE

OTHER

PERPETUAL

PLACE

PRIMARY

PRIMITIVE

SILLY

SIN

SOCKET

SPIRIT

SUFFER

URGED

VEX

VILE

VIOLATE

VIOLENCE

```
Y E P O P M G D C X J I A R J N Z
F N T U T C H U E S N I L Q I Z V
T G O U S G W V N I C J H A S T D
I Q B O R B E X C Z R W R G W S B
J F N I S B X R T E E X H H I E Z
X Z Y E L E J E H C U R W L U W Q
T E K C O S T T R G E H L R G N C
G G D W P A O E C F K Y K T F V G
Y V P E L L A H F K E Y V T R I U
S U U O V T A U P G T D N N I O Y
G P I R U O S C E Q I M P E G L D
O V I R G V L Y E L N A R M H E M
U P E R P E T U A L I V I G T N C
E T M D I Z D U L H F V M D F C B
Q H B W Q T P R W Q N B A U U E V
T P R I M I T I V E I J R J L C D
N T N E D I V E M Z V R Y E G Z F
```

Answers on page 185

"THE BLACK CAT" PT. 7

Every word listed is contained within the group of letters. Words can be found in a straight line horizontally, vertically, or diagonally. They may be read either forward or backward.

ACCURACY

ATROCITY

ATTRIBUTED

BLAZING

COMPARTMENT

CRUEL DEED

DENSE CROWD

DESPAIR

DISASTER

ENTIRE

ESCAPE

FIRE

FLAMES

GIGANTIC

GRAVEN

HEAD

IMPERFECT

PORTION

RESTED

ROPE

RUINS

STRANGE

WEAKNESS

WEALTH

```
T  R  I  E  H  D  R  A  J  D  S  D  K  R  D  O  G
H  C  E  O  G  U  I  E  V  A  Y  D  R  E  L  J  Y
B  L  A  Z  I  N  G  S  S  X  W  Z  T  G  X  U  C
U  J  Q  N  X  N  A  M  A  O  H  U  N  C  P  D  A
D  G  S  H  F  S  I  R  R  S  B  F  E  S  O  E  R
J  A  X  G  U  N  T  C  T  I  T  C  V  F  R  E  U
L  B  E  L  W  E  E  A  R  S  U  E  A  I  T  D  C
L  P  B  H  P  S  W  T  G  E  L  M  R  R  I  L  C
X  R  H  O  N  A  T  L  E  Y  S  S  G  E  O  E  A
W  I  R  E  R  A  T  S  C  P  J  T  B  P  N  U  X
E  A  D  R  Y  Z  C  L  E  O  L  W  E  Y  K  R  Z
A  P  K  Q  A  A  C  R  B  H  T  X  E  D  N  C  N
K  S  F  R  P  Q  I  F  L  A  M  E  S  A  E  Y  G
N  E  M  E  Y  T  I  C  O  R  T  A  J  S  L  B  P
E  D  X  I  N  I  M  P  E  R  F  E  C  T  A  T  P
S  T  N  E  M  T  R  A  P  M  O  C  J  F  M  S  H
S  G  I  G  A  N  T  I  C  O  U  I  L  D  E  X  P
```

Answers on page 185

Every word listed is contained within the group of letters. Words can be found in a straight line horizontally, vertically, or diagonally. They may be read either forward or backward.

ADJACENT

ALARM

ANIMAL

APPARITION

AROUSING

CARCASS

CAT

CHAMBER

CROWD

CRUELTY

EXTREME

FLAMES

GARDEN

HUNG

LIME

PLASTER

REFLECTION

SCARCELY

SLEEP

SUBSTANCE

TERROR

THROWN

TREE

VIEW

WONDER

```
B  T  D  E  I  H  B  Q  C  L  A  M  I  N  A  E  R
O  G  Q  L  M  A  P  P  A  R  I  T  I  O  N  O  F
V  R  Q  X  W  I  E  O  Y  L  T  J  F  D  R  K  T
S  E  M  A  L  F  L  T  Y  R  T  B  H  R  N  P  V
C  U  X  X  L  S  N  T  T  E  H  G  E  H  U  L  R
T  Y  B  Y  J  E  C  Q  R  F  R  T  T  G  S  A  Y
C  E  L  S  C  Q  Q  A  K  L  O  N  H  S  S  Z
P  I  A  A  T  G  C  K  R  E  W  N  E  O  A  T  B
N  E  J  R  T  A  C  H  Z  C  N  X  J  D  C  E  R
F  D  E  Z  O  R  N  P  I  T  E  E  C  T  R  R  D
A  A  H  L  Z  U  E  C  Z  I  K  L  D  R  A  A  E
S  S  Y  O  S  H  S  B  E  O  A  R  Y  B  C  M  G
D  W  O  N  D  E  R  I  M  N  Q  M  T  B  B  R  W
V  W  E  I  R  Q  W  H  N  A  U  B  R  C  F  A  Q
O  Y  O  I  L  N  U  C  L  G  H  W  E  O  H  L  W
E  F  P  R  V  Y  T  L  E  U  R  C  E  A  V  A  H
G  N  U  H  C  E  X  T  R  E  M  E  R  O  B  D  H
```

115

Answers on page 185

Every word listed is contained within the group of letters. Words can be found in a straight line horizontally, vertically, or diagonally. They may be read either forward or backward.

ACCOUNTED

ANIMAL

CAT

CONSCIENCE

DETAILED

FAIL

FANCY

HABITUALLY

HALF-SENTIMENT

IMPRESSION

MONTHS

PERIOD

PET

PHANTASM

PLACE

REASON

REGRET

REMORSE

SEEMED

SIMILAR

SPECIES

SPIRIT

STARTLING

SUPPLY

VILE HAUNTS

```
R  Y  I  M  P  R  E  S  S  I  O  N  J  B  O  G  B
C  L  D  L  I  H  P  C  O  N  S  C  I  E  N  C  E
L  L  C  E  K  Q  E  X  G  N  I  L  T  R  A  T  S
O  A  M  S  T  S  T  N  U  A  H  E  L  I  V  F  I
T  U  S  S  E  A  M  X  L  K  X  F  E  D  A  R  M
V  T  A  S  I  I  I  U  L  L  S  B  G  I  D  R  I
I  I  T  X  H  T  C  L  B  X  U  V  L  E  E  E  L
A  B  N  A  S  T  O  E  E  O  P  Q  C  G  M  G  A
V  A  A  L  N  D  N  N  P  D  P  A  K  S  E  R  R
D  H  H  O  I  Z  O  O  O  S  L  E  D  X  E  E  R
W  T  P  T  Q  S  U  T  M  P  Y  V  V  L  S  T  Z
A  S  S  D  A  X  A  C  C  O  U  N  T  E  D  L  P
Q  C  M  E  P  V  Y  N  S  P  I  R  I  T  S  H  E
E  S  R  O  M  E  R  G  I  T  F  H  O  U  R  K  R
O  T  A  Y  M  R  Q  O  T  M  X  J  Y  T  U  Y  I
Y  C  N  A  F  C  D  G  A  O  A  S  T  W  Z  R  O
S  T  N  E  M  I  T  N  E  S  F  L  A  H  D  M  D
```

Answers on page 186

Every word listed is contained within the group of letters. Words can be found in a straight line horizontally, vertically, or diagonally. They may be read either forward or backward.

ATTENTION	INFAMY
BLACK CAT	NIGHT
BLACK OBJECT	PERCEIVED
CHIEF	PLUTO
CONSTITUTED	PORTION
COVERING	REGION
DEN	RESEMBLING
DRAWN	RESPECT
GIN	RUM
HEAD	STEADILY
HOGSHEAD	STUPEFIED
IMMENSE	SURPRISE
INDEFINITE	TOUCHED

```
S  L  G  O  Z  C  O  N  S  T  I  T  U  T  E  D  H
T  N  O  N  R  E  S  P  E  C  T  W  A  X  E  Z  P
U  K  I  K  I  T  E  Q  S  I  C  C  Y  G  S  K  E
P  O  R  Q  R  L  N  F  X  R  K  T  H  N  I  L  R
E  I  E  M  W  F  B  W  K  C  O  H  B  I  R  L  C
F  U  F  N  M  Y  J  M  A  L  F  C  L  R  P  P  E
I  E  Z  K  M  D  C  L  E  R  J  L  A  E  R  O  I
E  W  I  A  K  R  B  Q  Q  S  D  D  C  V  U  R  V
D  A  F  H  K  E  S  M  E  O  E  Q  K  O  S  T  E
V  N  T  J  C  G  S  A  Z  H  Z  R  O  C  A  I  D
I  B  R  T  J  I  C  K  C  C  E  J  B  I  R  O  B
N  M  P  M  E  O  C  U  Y  B  S  T  J  P  Z  N  N
I  V  T  U  L  N  O  E  L  C  N  A  E  L  E  I  J
G  X  H  R  D  T  T  J  R  D  E  O  C  U  G  A  H
H  W  S  T  E  A  D  I  L  Y  M  Q  T  T  N  E  D
T  X  D  A  E  H  S  G  O  H  M  L  S  O  A  U  I
Y  E  T  I  N  I  F  E  D  N  I  B  I  D  X  I  I
```

119

Answers on page 186

"THE BLACK CAT" PT. 11

Every word listed is contained within the group of letters. Words can be found in a straight line horizontally, vertically, or diagonally. They may be read either forward or backward.

ANIMAL

BEFORE

CARESSES

CLAIM

CONTINUED

CREATURE

HAND

IMMEDIATELY

LANDLORD

NOTHING

NOTICE

OFFERED

PATTING

PERMITTED

PERSON

PREPARED

PURCHASE

PURRED

RUBBED

SEARCH

STOOPING

TOUCHING

```
Y  V  W  Q  Y  C  J  O  F  F  E  R  E  D  C  X  C
L  G  N  I  P  O  O  T  S  I  M  S  Z  E  Y  S  N
G  Y  R  J  E  D  E  R  A  P  E  R  P  B  L  O  N
C  Q  M  Z  R  O  R  M  E  S  T  D  D  B  E  P  F
O  S  X  G  S  G  V  R  S  O  D  E  E  U  T  H  S
N  P  L  T  O  D  M  E  U  Z  R  U  R  R  A  E  Q
E  X  U  P  N  I  R  C  V  K  J  N  R  D  I  Z  X
S  L  G  H  T  A  H  N  A  J  B  I  U  R  D  U  F
A  A  V  T  C  I  S  G  O  A  Z  T  P  O  E  P  U
H  T  E  F  N  E  P  E  N  T  Z  N  Z  L  M  N  H
C  D  J  G  N  W  R  I  A  I  I  O  C  D  M  J  M
R  K  T  Q  P  O  M  U  U  R  T  C  H  N  I  I  H
U  G  V  P  F  A  Y  H  T  E  C  T  E  A  A  A  T
P  V  J  E  L  U  X  F  L  A  X  H  A  L  N  Q  P
Z  T  B  Y  X  T  L  C  F  W  E  O  C  P  Q  D  X
N  O  T  H  I  N  G  G  G  X  X  R  X  V  N  Z  A
O  U  T  J  L  F  Y  M  U  V  I  X  C  X  Y  V  B
```

Answers on page 186

121

Every word listed is contained within the group of letters. Words can be found in a straight line horizontally, vertically, or diagonally. They may be read either forward or backward.

ABUSING

ANNOYED

ARISING

AVOIDED

CREATURE

CRUELTY

DEED

DISGUSTED

DISLIKE

FEELINGS

FONDNESS

HATRED

HOW

KNOW

LOATHING

ODIOUS

PART

PESTILENCE

REVERSE

SHAME

SILENTLY

STRIKE

VIOLENTLY

```
O R L X G Y G R F D X B H P A R T
D E E D K N Z L E O P E U L Q Y U
Q U W N I G S Y B Y M Z L M A F P
T A O S X L O U V G A B T V H E F
R W U V L N E D O I R O O M Q E O
G B G I N N M D I I O I S I P L N
A G N A V B A E F S D L S J E I D
E N I R Z P H T K E L O E N R N N
S I H L I W S S D I V I F N U G E
R S T A G P I U O X R Q K B T S S
E I A D H L C G U E H T R E A L S
V R O H E R T S A F X J S W E A Y
E A L N U R J I C K W L O N R V T
R W T E X M T D O B C H N L C C S
K L L A Q J W A B X R D E S R T R
Y T L X L T B M H J A L Y Z G C Q
Y P E S T I L E N C E F M Q H P Y
```

Answers on page 186

"THE BLACK CAT" PT. 13

Every word listed is contained within the group of letters. Words can be found in a straight line horizontally, vertically, or diagonally. They may be read either forward or backward.

ADDED

BEAST

BROUGHT

CIRCUMSTANCE

DEPRIVED

DISCOVERY

DOUBT

ENDEARED

EYES

FEELING

HATRED

HIGH

HUMANITY

MORNING

ONCE BEEN

PLUTO

POSSESSED

PUREST PLEASURES

SIMPLEST

SOURCE

TRAIT

WIFE

```
P U R E S T P L E A S U R E S W A
J D R K D G E Z F G E E D D I J S
C T W R X E Q I D T X K O F M A I
S O U R C E R H T N H T E O D D M
Q U T D I S I T N P T G R O E E P
X B V U X D O N A D O N U S P V L
I M T Y L E Y H P H I B S O F X E
H V R C D P V C Y N T E P I R S S
I B A J I R X P G F S E S V E B T
G M I V S I X E C S N A E Y Q K A
H N T C C V C J O E N D E A R E D
X K I F O E K P W H L D A B L W D
C H J L V D W N E E B E C N O G T
G T N X E D Z I K F Z D X K G G S
Y G P G R E G X Y T I N A M U H A
P O F H Y B F K I X G I G M K U E
B A R C I R C U M S T A N C E Z B
```

Answers on page 187

"THE BLACK CAT" PT. 14

Every word listed is contained within the group of letters. Words can be found in a straight line horizontally, vertically, or diagonally. They may be read either forward or backward.

AROSE

AVERSION

BETWEEN

BLOW

BREAST

CHAIR

CLAMBER

CONFESS

CRIME

CROUCH

DESTROY

DIFFICULT

DREAD

FASTENING

FOOTSTEPS

INCREASE

KNEES

LOATHSOME

LONG

LONGED

MANNER

MEMORY

PARTIALITY

PERTINACITY

READER

SHARP CLAWS

```
C  Y  S  D  Y  S  Q  N  O  I  S  R  E  V  A  F  K
T  O  P  U  R  L  T  Y  D  I  F  F  I  C  U  L  T
A  R  N  C  O  B  U  T  Y  W  T  X  R  Z  Q  P  L
R  T  D  F  M  Q  X  I  S  P  E  T  S  T  O  O  F
O  S  A  H  E  C  Y  C  Y  W  U  G  S  I  A  H  A
S  E  H  G  M  S  R  A  I  F  O  A  J  T  O  O  S
E  D  G  C  M  N  S  N  Q  P  E  C  H  A  I  R  T
D  L  G  P  A  H  C  I  T  R  J  S  R  B  O  Y  E
L  B  L  C  G  R  K  T  B  A  O  Z  E  E  D  T  N
O  S  X  H  E  V  H  R  S  M  S  N  N  T  S  I  I
N  G  E  A  T  C  E  E  P  X  W  N  W  U  L  N
G  H  S  E  U  J  D  P  Y  A  U  Q  A  E  M  A  G
P  E  H  O  N  J  N  R  R  S  D  T  M  E  J  I  N
V  V  R  B  I  K  E  M  I  R  C  E  G  N  H  T  Z
K  C  L  Y  G  C  L  A  M  B  E  R  R  X  P  R  Y
L  O  N  G  E  D  R  B  F  T  P  T  D  R  E  A  D
W  Q  S  W  A  L  C  P  R  A  H  S  E  W  Q  P  U
```

Answers on page 187

"THE BLACK CAT" PT. 15

Every word listed is contained within the group of letters. Words can be found in a straight line horizontally, vertically, or diagonally. They may be read either forward or backward.

ASHAMED

BEAST

CHIMERAS

CONCEIVE

CRIME

DEATH

DEFINE

DEGREES

DESTROYED

DREAD

DREADED

FANCIFUL

GALLOWS

HIDEOUS

HORROR

INDEFINITE

INSPIRED

LOATHED

MARK

MONSTER

OBJECT

PHYSICAL

REASON

RIGOROUS

TERROR

VISIBLE

WHITE HAIR

```
S D E D A E R D D E S T R O Y E D
G E L A H I D E O U S Z L H R H D
F B E E C D U N F A N C I F U L C
G L Y R L T D E M A H S A D Z E X
F M I D G Z X H P O P Q B E R U K
Q M E P D E O W H T N F U F G Y B
E V D U M R D S Y O L S L I J F H
L B K G R Z W E S M D J T N S T D
B E M O E O V U I T E O Z E A W F
I A R U L I O E C K R B B E R I R
S S L L E R L E A M I S D P E C W
I T A C O O J Q L M P T E R R O R
V G N G A B H Q N O S A E R X E G
K O I T O P I F X P N J T F Z S N
C R H I N I N D E F I N I T E D Z
S E A C H I M E R A S F S C O U G
D W Z M W P D C R I A H E T I H W
```

Answers on page 187

129

Every word listed is contained within the group of letters. Words can be found in a straight line horizontally, vertically, or diagonally. They may be read either forward or backward.

BREATH

BRUTE BEAST

CONTEMPTUOUSLY

CREATURE

DREAMS

ETERNALLY

FASHIONED

FELLOW

FORMER

HEART

HIGH GOD

HOURLY

HUMANITY

INCARNATE

INSUFFERABLE

MOMENT

POWER

REST

SHAKE

THING

UNUTTERABLE

WEIGHT

WRETCHED

```
B I S G V L B D F O R M E R M T B
V T I N S U F F E R A B L E U Y R
Z S E R J J G J L E E W H W L Y E
U E T P O W E R L K F R E S L R A
N R A D B Y O L O A T O U I C Q T
U G N V E K G C W H D O G H G I H
T B R X B N I T A S U O A G C H O
T T A X C Y O Y E T B T O L C I T
E I C D L A T I P K S L G J K M H
R T N S E I P M H A J S K R C O T
A M I T N H E Q E S M L T J R N H
B K H A B T C B P A A L P R E C I
L E M O N W E T E F I F J M A B N
E U J O U T U R E A R A O X T E G
H F C U U R D B W R Q M K Z U Y H
E T E R N A L L Y O W S X V R C Z
V Y B I X Y B Y Z D T E I I E K I
```

Answers on page 187

"THE BLACK CAT" PT. 17

Every word listed is contained within the group of letters. Words can be found in a straight line horizontally, vertically, or diagonally. They may be read either forward or backward.

BENEATH

BLINDLY

DARKEST

FEEBLE

FREQUENT

FURY

GOOD

HATRED

INCREASED

INTIMATES

MANKIND

MOODINESS

MOST EVIL

MYSELF

PATIENT

PRESSURE

SUCCUMBED

SUFFERERS

THOUGHTS

TORMENTS

UNCOMPLAINING

UNGOVERNABLE

USUAL

```
U N G O V E R N A B L E M H Z H U
Q X M A N K I N D O X S O L C T N
P R E S S U R E F U T R O A N A C
T I N C R E A S E D H E D U M D O
Z S F Z Q B P A C I O R I S D V M
N A E E M A E N T A U E N U Y S P
W Z H K T U D D V K G F E W M M L
I K A I R M E W F S H F S U R Q A
Y A E C D A B J K A T U S B C F I
I N C F Z Y D J T B S S T E H R N
T O U T R V L R F B M Z U T T E I
M R A C X O E E L B E E F P A Q N
Y I M V C D E B M U C C U S E U G
S T N E M R O T H C L Q Q U N E V
E H D O O G B L I N D L Y X E N X
L H M O S T E V I L D D Q C B T R
F M I N T I M A T E S P K Z E N N
```

Answers on page 188

133

"THE BLACK CAT" PT. 18

Every word listed is contained within the group of letters. Words can be found in a straight line horizontally, vertically, or diagonally. They may be read either forward or backward.

ACCOMPANIED

ANIMAL

ARRESTED

AXE

BLOW

BRAIN

CHILDISH

DEMONIACAL

DESCENDED

FORGETTING

GOADED

GRASP

GROAN

HAND

HEADLONG

HOUSEHOLD

INHABIT

INSTANTLY

INTERFERENCE

MADNESS

POVERTY

STEEP

WITHDREW

WRATH

```
V U V T B X G Y E Z L O I A I B I
F L B L A C A I N O M E D N I J G
W P O S Z W Y W G O B D T U F B R
X W T H X W I H O U S E H O L D O
Y L T N A T S N I W R G H E Y W A
D L E Z H I G S R F O R E O U S N
C R U D D H D A E A J A A L P A P
N P R L A Y T R D G D S D B C J J
X E I N W H E E R I W P L C T D T
W H D D F N D A G L W T O A A E S
C R M E C B L X M E K M N R B S G
P P B E J M B E N Y P I G R G C P
Z J F Z S S E N D A M R A E W E O
J D G S M D E F N A S I M S E N P
I N H A B I T I L J N P F T K D F
Y C F O R G E T T I N G S E T E J
H N G W T D Y T R E V O P D V D C
```

135

Answers on page 188

"THE BLACK CAT" PT. 19

Every word listed is contained within the group of letters. Words can be found in a straight line horizontally, vertically, or diagonally. They may be read either forward or backward.

ACCOMPLISHED

CELLAR

CONCEALING

CONSIDERED

CORPSE

CUTTING

DAY

DETERMINED

ENTIRE

EXPEDIENT

FIRE

GRAVE

HIDEOUS

HOUSE

MERCHANDIZE

MIDDLE AGES

MONKS

NEIGHBORS

NIGHT

OBSERVED

PORTER

PROJECTS

RECORDED

REMOVE

WALLED

```
Z  P  W  S  C  I  A  P  R  O  J  E  C  T  S  R  V
C  C  C  G  S  X  H  D  G  X  L  D  P  N  S  M  R
U  O  K  I  U  U  I  M  M  Z  C  E  W  E  H  I  E
T  N  B  D  M  F  D  X  X  P  Z  N  B  I  K  D  C
T  C  T  I  E  H  E  V  M  Y  I  I  M  D  S  D  O
I  E  O  C  S  D  O  K  B  G  Y  M  E  E  R  L  R
N  A  M  H  E  S  U  O  H  W  E  R  R  P  O  E  D
G  L  V  H  C  L  S  T  E  R  E  E  C  X  B  A  E
Y  I  C  Z  Y  J  F  V  I  D  V  T  H  E  H  G  D
O  N  O  T  K  J  O  F  I  F  Z  E  A  O  G  E  M
B  G  R  G  S  M  B  S  G  G  P  D  N  P  I  S  N
S  G  P  A  E  H  N  K  E  S  O  F  D  E  E  W  M
E  T  S  R  L  O  K  N  B  N  R  I  I  W  N  A  T
R  A  E  U  C  L  D  O  K  W  T  S  Z  R  X  L  T
V  Y  L  H  G  A  E  M  V  A  E  I  E  P  Y  L  K
E  M  Q  E  Y  Z  V  C  P  D  R  G  R  A  V  E  G
D  E  H  S  I  L  P  M  O  C  C  A  Y  E  O  D  S
```

Answers on page 188

"THE BLACK CAT" PT. 20

Every word listed is contained within the group of letters. Words can be found in a straight line horizontally, vertically, or diagonally. They may be read either forward or backward.

ADAPTED

ATMOSPHERE

BRICKS

CELLAR

CHIMNEY

CORPSE

DAMPNESS

DETECT

DISPLACE

DOUBT

FIREPLACE

HARDENING

INSERT

LOOSELY

PLASTERED

PREVENTED

PROJECTION

PURPOSE

READILY

RESEMBLE

REST

ROUGH

SUSPICIOUS

WHOLE

```
U  A  R  K  X  Y  N  J  D  B  O  Z  D  V  T  F  C
V  R  A  R  G  V  M  E  W  E  S  I  N  S  E  R  T
S  F  W  M  N  Z  D  E  R  E  T  S  A  L  P  C  S
V  S  U  T  C  E  T  E  D  H  V  P  P  P  E  Z  W
E  U  R  E  S  T  H  K  L  K  R  E  A  D  I  L  Y
E  S  O  P  R  U  P  R  G  N  I  N  E  D  R  A  H
R  P  D  E  T  N  E  V  E  R  P  W  B  G  A  U  N
E  I  Z  V  I  T  C  E  S  V  D  R  O  F  U  K  O
H  C  S  K  G  O  E  M  T  P  X  D  O  R  L  F  I
P  I  Z  K  E  E  L  B  M  E  S  E  R  U  P  F  T
S  O  Z  R  C  C  L  O  C  O  R  P  S  E  G  V  C
O  U  X  K  F  I  A  O  O  M  T  B  U  O  D  H  E
M  S  C  M  U  J  R  L  M  S  U  R  S  O  I  O  J
T  M  D  W  S  M  K  B  P  X  E  K  Q  M  P  L  O
A  E  L  O  H  W  A  U  B  S  B  L  N  P  I  W  R
P  N  S  S  E  N  P  M  A  D  I  E  Y  A  I  W  P
F  I  R  E  P  L  A  C  E  B  Y  D  R  H  K  K  U
```

Answers on page 188

Every word listed is contained within the group of letters. Words can be found in a straight line horizontally, vertically, or diagonally. They may be read either forward or backward.

BRICKS

CALCULATION

CAREFULLY

CROWBAR

DECEIVED

DEPOSITED

DISLODGED

DISTINGUISHED

DISTURBED

FINISHED

FLOOR

LABOR

LOOKED

MINUTEST

MORTAR

MYSELF

ORIGINALLY

POSITION

PRECAUTION

RUBBISH

SATISFIED

SLIGHTEST

TRIUMPHANTLY

TROUBLE

```
E C S L I G H T E S T K L Z M U J
L D K R Y P Z T S E T U N I M E K
D I C P O X O R I G I N A L L Y K
E S I T R I U M P H A N T L Y D J
K T R Z N T M O R T A R D H C E V
O I B Z B S U A R M K E G N A I Q
O N Q D V R B R N G C M O D R F L
L G K A R W O Z O E K I E H E S U
D U Q C O O D V I U T G D S F I M
E I L R L T B V T U D I P I U T F
P S C F O B E A A O S T O B L A I
O H I C G D W C L T M R S B L S N
S E X V H S E S U Q Y O I U Y K I
I D U U L R I R C T S U T R Z L S
T S H F P D B B L A E B I G Z R H
E Q S H Z E W Q A H L L O I Q X E
D Z M B D C A Y C K F E N E F A D
```

Answers on page 189

Every word listed is contained within the group of letters. Words can be found in a straight line horizontally, vertically, or diagonally. They may be read either forward or backward.

ABSENCE	FELICITY
ALARMED	FREEMAN
BEAST	LENGTH
BOSOM	MOMENT
BREATHED	MONSTER
BURDEN	MOOD
CRAFTY	NOTHING
DEATH	PREMISES
DESCRIBE	SECOND
DOUBT	THIRD
FATE	VIOLENCE

G H P P R B D N A C C S F Y Z K V
B O U D P L K M O M E N T S O Y H
T U Y D E S C R I B E D M O W C N
T R W N R E I X Z Z P O X P R P N
I X G D A F N S N Y Z U G A H N A
I T V I O L E N C E Y B F R C A M
H C A W F E D O A H H T D P G H E
E L Z A S H U Z T A Y E N R N T E
U N T I C E C D T Y M A Z E I A R
F E E J A O C Q E R P W Y M H E F
E P G D Z D Q O A Z Z V V I T D J
L D F P R P K L N I J M O S O B B
I F O P I U A P W D K R L E N Y H
C N R O M A B S E N C E T S H R N
I C S P M B R E A T H E D R I H T
T M O N S T E R J K P V M X G I Z
Y T L S B G C T S A E B R H B F E

Answers on page 189

"THE BLACK CAT" PT. 23

Every word listed is contained within the group of letters. Words can be found in a straight line horizontally, vertically, or diagonally. They may be read either forward or backward.

BOSOM	OFFICERS
CALMLY	PARTY
CELLAR	PLACE
CORNER	POLICE
FOLDED	PREMISES
FOURTH	PREPARED
HEART	RENDER
HOUSE	RIGOROUS
LENGTH	SLUMBERS
MUSCLE	THIRD
NOOK	TRIUMPH

```
D  P  A  G  D  O  S  B  A  C  Y  E  N  V  T  V  S
R  R  I  G  O  R  O  U  S  T  Z  D  I  E  O  E  J
I  C  M  K  W  F  S  L  U  M  B  E  R  S  F  C  T
H  O  O  M  C  O  X  Y  D  L  O  I  X  I  F  A  M
T  R  S  I  E  U  T  A  Q  L  E  D  X  X  I  L  T
B  N  O  F  K  R  J  M  E  S  Y  O  D  R  C  P  A
X  E  B  F  I  T  L  R  U  P  A  L  Q  M  E  I  G
O  R  U  U  I  H  E  Y  U  S  U  R  M  Q  R  V  M
G  N  M  J  G  D  N  T  S  G  C  A  O  L  S  F  M
Y  P  P  O  N  S  G  A  E  G  L  L  J  D  A  J  C
H  T  C  E  F  R  T  W  S  T  L  L  E  N  P  C  W
D  P  R  F  V  E  H  B  I  Q  U  E  X  Z  E  B  P
I  E  C  A  C  J  X  R  M  J  Y  C  J  N  O  O  K
F  S  T  I  P  T  R  A  E  H  B  E  I  R  T  O  M
K  U  L  U  R  N  J  K  R  Y  Z  J  W  F  W  A  Q
Z  O  F  O  L  D  E  D  P  D  E  R  A  P  E  R  P
P  H  V  J  Z  K  P  F  P  Z  U  O  W  I  F  V  X
```

Answers on page 189

Every word listed is contained within the group of letters. Words can be found in a straight line horizontally, vertically, or diagonally. They may be read either forward or backward.

ALLAYED

ASCENDED

BEHIND

BOSOM

BRAVADO

CANE

CONSTRUCTED

CORPSE

COURTESY

DELIGHT

EASILY

EXCELLENTLY

FRENZY

GENTLEMEN

HAND

HEALTH

HEAVILY

KNEW

PORTION

RABID

SOLIDLY

STOOD

SUSPICIONS

UTTERED

WALLS

```
I  X  I  B  I  C  J  Y  W  Y  C  G  G  S  E  B  N
G  G  V  R  V  Y  Z  N  E  R  F  D  H  E  R  H  E
C  K  W  A  D  D  C  S  D  M  E  S  F  Q  Y  D  M
F  B  G  V  N  I  O  R  C  Z  O  B  D  L  N  E  E
N  A  Q  A  A  B  R  D  Y  E  W  S  T  I  E  T  L
E  F  C  D  H  A  P  L  O  G  A  N  O  Q  O  C  T
T  A  G  O  S  R  S  N  B  O  E  S  A  B  U  U  N
D  S  O  I  Y  N  E  E  O  L  T  L  I  U  V  R  E
N  C  Y  T  J  N  C  F  L  I  L  S  E  L  A  T  G
I  E  N  A  C  K  M  E  X  A  T  G  C  K  Y  S  Z
H  N  E  W  N  S  C  Y  Y  L  M  R  L  Z  L  N  U
E  D  P  E  Y  X  U  E  L  Q  H  L  O  L  M  O  T
B  E  W  P  E  P  D  A  Y  D  R  E  A  P  J  C  T
N  D  J  T  H  G  I  L  E  D  I  W  A  R  O  S  E
Y  S  E  T  R  U  O  C  G  C  F  L  U  L  C  D  R
S  N  O  I  C  I  P  S  U  S  Q  L  O  I  T  F  E
M  H  Y  L  I  V  A  E  H  Q  S  J  U  S  N  H  D
```

Answers on page 189

147

Every word listed is contained within the group of letters. Words can be found in a straight line horizontally, vertically, or diagonally. They may be read either forward or backward.

AGONY

ARISEN

BLOWS

BROKEN

CRY

DELIVER

DEMONS

EXULT

FANGS

HORROR

HOWL

INHUMAN

LOUD

MUFFLED

QUICKLY

SHIELD

SILENCE

SOBBING

SOONER

THROATS

TOMB

TRIUMPH

VOICE

```
P  A  K  N  H  T  R  I  U  M  P  H  L  M  B  X  Y
T  E  G  L  S  B  Y  U  N  R  I  A  N  T  W  B  S
T  O  L  W  T  I  J  G  O  F  W  E  L  Y  Z  R  O
D  B  M  N  A  I  E  R  Q  C  S  U  T  V  N  O  B
C  O  B  B  O  G  R  B  M  I  X  O  O  U  R  K  B
Q  F  M  Q  R  O  N  P  R  E  V  I  O  L  N  E  I
N  A  M  U  H  N  I  A  S  Q  C  D  Z  N  D  N  N
V  N  R  I  T  E  I  S  J  E  L  D  Z  P  E  B  G
L  G  I  C  M  C  Q  K  D  E  W  B  E  F  R  R  X
W  S  X  K  X  N  Q  Y  I  E  E  H  M  M  D  C  D
O  R  B  L  A  E  X  H  H  E  L  I  F  S  O  A  K
H  E  E  Y  G  L  S  H  V  O  X  F  B  J  C  N  H
X  V  F  U  F  I  M  Q  X  B  H  T  F  A  S  Y  S
P  I  N  M  P  S  E  L  L  L  S  M  G  U  R  O  X
L  L  U  M  F  M  O  O  E  X  O  O  C  M  I  L
Z  E  R  H  L  U  W  F  V  P  N  O  A  E  Y  J  J
K  D  Q  G  D  S  G  V  J  Y  N  J  X  A  G  M  J
```

Answers on page 190

Every word listed is contained within the group of letters. Words can be found in a straight line horizontally, vertically, or diagonally. They may be read either forward or backward. Leftover letters will reveal an interesting bit of trivia about Poe's legend.

CLOTTED	MOTIONLESS
CONSIGNED	MURDER
CORPSE	OPPOSITE
CRAFT	SEDUCED
DECAYED	SOLITARY
DOZEN	SPECTATORS
ERECT	STAGGERED
EXTENDED	STAIRS
EXTREMITY	SWOONING
FOLLY	TERROR
HIDEOUS	THOUGHTS
INFORMING	TOILING
INSTANT	TOMB
MONSTER	

```
Y  L  L  O  F  T  H  E  E  B  B  N  L  A  C  K  C
A  T  W  G  A  S  F  I  X  M  R  E  S  T  P  U  B
L  M  O  N  S  T  E  R  T  O  I  Z  S  H  E  D  E
G  I  N  I  T  S  H  G  E  T  S  O  E  S  S  R  S
N  A  T  M  P  U  R  D  N  E  A  D  Y  T  E  T  E
I  M  U  R  D  E  R  V  D  I  E  N  H  C  A  I  N
L  G  O  O  P  O  S  U  E  T  N  G  T  I  O  H  N
I  C  A  F  U  C  C  G  D  U  U  O  R  S  I  D  T
O  1  9  N  1  E  O  8  E  O  4  S  O  D  3  E  E
T  T  H  I  D  E  S  N  H  T  R  T  E  W  O  T  X
R  Y  H  A  T  N  A  T  S  N  I  O  S  B  S  T  T
S  T  A  G  G  E  R  E  D  I  U  S  R  E  C  O  R
M  O  T  I  O  N  L  E  S  S  G  E  O  R  N  L  E
S  P  E  C  T  A  T  O  R  S  P  N  A  P  E  C  M
A  R  O  D  I  E  D  A  N  D  A  F  E  D  P  T  I
A  P  D  E  C  A  Y  E  D  T  T  E  D  D  M  O  T
A  N  Y  T  I  M  S  O  L  I  T  A  R  Y  E  S  Y
```

Hidden Message: _____

_____

Answers on page 190

"SONNET—TO SCIENCE"

Every word listed is contained within the group of letters. Words can be found in a straight line horizontally, vertically, or diagonally. They may be read either forward or backward. Leftover letters will reveal an interesting bit of trivia about Poe's legend.

ALBEIT

ALTEREST

DAUGHTER

DRAGGED

DRIVEN

FLOOD

GREEN GRASS

HAMADRYAD

JEWELLED

NAIAD

OLD TIME

PREYEST

REALITIES

SCIENCE

SHELTER

SOARED

SUMMER

TREASURE

UNDAUNTED

VULTURE

WANDERING

WINGS

WOOD

```
S O N S R E T H G U A D N E T T O
S C I E G N C H S E I T I L A E R
N A I A D N E W A E C N E I C S A
S P T U B L I I V M S O H E D I N
P O E R S S E W C U A L O N D C O
G L L D E E C T I O L D R I V E N
R N O E F A P A O E T T R R Y A S
E P L L A A S R L S A I U Y A O F
E R I L N 1 8 U H T 2 M 9 R A W U
N E H E I C H E R W E E A R E D N
G Y S W T H L T D E W R E E F I D
R E R E S T R I T O O D E P U B A
A S L J E I C E A T O I O S N T U
S T H R A T P B M O D L E D T I N
S D N T U S E L T M H E F P E N T
G N I R E D N A W N U A M E A B E
O S T O D R A G G E D S N I A N D
```

Hidden Message: _____

_____

Answers on page 190

153

"A DREAM"

Every word listed is contained within the group of letters. Words can be found in a straight line horizontally, vertically, or diagonally. They may be read either forward or backward.

BROKEN-HEARTED

CAST

CHEERED

CHIDING

DARK NIGHT

DAY

DREAMED

GUIDING

HOLY DREAM

JOY DEPARTED

LIGHT

LONELY

LOVELY BEAM

PAST

PURELY BRIGHT

RAY

STORM

THINGS

TREMBLED

TRUTH'S

TURNED

VISIONS

WAKING

WORLD

```
I  T  H  G  I  R  B  Y  L  E  R  U  P  U  D  Y  G
J  O  Y  D  E  P  A  R  T  E  D  H  P  S  A  G  Z
U  T  R  E  M  B  L  E  D  T  W  E  N  S  U  X  M
A  Y  O  N  B  X  L  F  L  K  H  O  R  I  D  A  D
A  S  Z  R  G  N  I  K  A  W  I  T  D  E  E  L  U
S  U  H  U  I  P  V  U  H  S  O  I  T  R  E  V  H
Y  C  A  T  D  B  M  G  I  C  N  R  D  B  T  H  G
B  L  H  T  U  I  T  V  C  G  A  Y  L  P  C  K  C
B  G  E  G  E  R  N  N  D  E  L  W  X  D  H  D  L
T  S  G  N  I  H  T  N  H  O  V  U  R  W  I  R  V
U  E  X  V  O  D  B  N  H  M  E  G  V  X  D  E  Q
M  A  E  B  Y  L  E  V  O  L  S  T  Q  X  I  A  L
C  X  D  A  R  K  N  I  G  H  T  T  H  Q  N  M  L
L  A  H  R  O  N  Z  O  J  B  P  N  O  G  G  E  L
D  N  Q  R  Y  Y  T  U  H  R  A  G  D  R  I  D  B
Z  A  B  Z  A  N  Y  D  A  G  S  P  S  H  M  L  O
R  M  Y  V  G  L  G  Y  M  Y  T  Y  C  A  S  T  J
```

Answers on page 190

"ELDORADO"

Every word listed is contained within the group of letters. Words can be found in a straight line horizontally, vertically, or diagonally. They may be read either forward or backward. Leftover letters will reveal an interesting bit of trivia about Poe's legend.

BOLD	LAND
BOLDLY	LENGTH
DOWN	MOON
ELDORADO	MOUNTAINS
FELL	PILGRIM
FOUND	REPLIED
GAILY	SHADOW
GALLANT KNIGHT	SINGING
GREW OLD	STRENGTH
GROUND	SUNSHINE
HEART	VALLEY
JOURNEYED	

```
D D E L W D O R A Y D O W A S F I
N N B R S O T P U L B L H I S H E
A U O D G I D N A I B S F E V O S
L O L T O N N A W A E U E E A K L
Y F D O N A I P H G R N I L L R 2
1 1 L D 8 4 9 G C S S S O N L L T
S C Y U L R D R N T E H N T E W I
N E T H T O H E R I E I C A Y P L
I I L F D O B E Y R S N N I I R A
A G O D L O N D R E U E S L H E T
T H E P O G W O E M N R G E C P O
N U N T T R S N T H G R E W O L D
U E L H O O A S T M I Y U T H I I
O C A L N U A D T M I V E O C E O
M L O M B N I A O O N C I T J D Y
M A D E O D F A L O L E N G T H L
G G A L L A N T K N I G H T O L D
```

Hidden Message: _____

_____

"THE RAVEN" PT.1

Every word listed is contained within the group of letters. Words can be found in a straight line horizontally, vertically, or diagonally. They may be read either forward or backward.

ANGELS

BEATING

CHAMBER DOOR

DECEMBER

DYING EMBER

ENTRANCE

ENTREATING

EVERMORE

FANTASTIC

GHOST

LOST LENORE

MIDNIGHT

MUTTERED

NAMELESS

NOTHING MORE

ONCE

PURPLE

QUAINT

RADIANT MAIDEN

RAPPING

REPEATING

RUSTLING

TAPPING

THRILLED

VISITER

WEARY

```
R A D I A N T M A I D E N D N H U R U
W D Y I N G E M B E R O T N U F Y Y A
J P E D E U B Y M A N E A P B Q T N R
Z S C Z R W T B B C B M Y D O X M X E
R C N F O G G H E O E X K Q O S U V P
M H A A M Z N Q G L M Q U A I N T I E
I A R N G D I I E I H D W R R E T S A
E M T T N E B S P C N K E B B V E I T
Z B N A I C S L T P Z D T B L E R T I
T E E S H E N T R E A T I N G R E E N
A R G T T M C Y N L S R Z M J M D R G
P D N I O B I D I I J G B B Y O M L J
P O I C N E O Z P D N H X J B R U A P
I O T Z E R A U U K A O L D F E A D A
N R A D E L L I R H T S S W F J U E P
G A E O X U K T P R U T A C G O U N W
U Y B W R U O Z L E F H Q Y S N X O T
S L E G N A W K E L O S T L E N O R E
E D L N Q R U S T L I N G X B P H N F
```

Answers on page 191

"THE RAVEN" PT. 2

Every word listed is contained within the group of letters. Words can be found in a straight line horizontally, vertically, or diagonally. They may be read either forward or backward.

BURNING

CHAMBER

DARKNESS

DOUBTING

DREAM

EXPLORE

FAINTLY

FORGIVENESS

HESITATING

LOUDER

MORTAL

MURMURED

MYSTERY

NAPPING

NOTHING MORE

OPENED

PEERING

RAPPING

SCARCE

SILENCE

SOUL

TAPPING

UNBROKEN

WHISPERED WORD

WINDOW LATTICE

```
Q O H G O X M N M C E N L C W K H
G N I N R U B P H X A P G I G L E
O U E I H J X A P P N W N X N B S
D N L P M N M L P E M D B U I K I
R O Y P D B O I C Y O K C A P W T
O T L A E R N N S W I A E F P N A
W H T R E G E T L F M O R T A L T
D I N S F L E A U O H L P U T D I
E N I R I R T O M R U C H A Z E N
R G A S Y T D R M G L O U D E R G
E M F K I T W O D I Q M P R G U N
P O X C C M M L L V X V K E N M I
S R E U N B R O K E N O W C I R T
I E N E S D A R K N E S S R R U B
H N I S G O P G K E X H O A E M U
W B D A S T U Q T S C X Z C E C O
D E N E P O V L Y S L V J S P U D
```

Answers on page 191

Every word listed is contained within the group of letters. Words can be found in a straight line horizontally, vertically, or diagonally. They may be read either forward or backward.

AGREEING

BEAST

BEGUILING

BIRD

BLESSED

CHAMBER DOOR

COUNTENANCE

DECORUM

DISCOURSE

FLIRT

FLUTTER

GHASTLY GRIM

HUMAN BEING

MEANING

NEVERMORE

OBEISANCE

PERCHED

RAVEN

RELEVANCY

SCULPTURED

SHUTTER

UNGAINLY

WANDERING

```
E H N I R N X X U N G A I N L Y E
S F A G R E E I N G B E A S T E U
R H T D H S L V H D D R I B S J Y
U V M M O A C E E J J S A F S T F
O P H Z B R S U R F W Y V P W O
C I M E H E J T L A M A V G E A C
S B T K O T G G L P N O J U R N O
I T S R G T V U W Y T C R E C D U
D R R L Z U X M I N G U Y E H E N
W B E I N L S E U L E R R O E R T
G D L T L F M I V R I H I E D I E
N F Q E T F A Z U D O N S M D N N
I H Q L S U G K V I O C G I T G A
N R D Y T S H U M A N B E I N G N
A R Y X U O E S M Z V Q C D W K C
E I G V X O M D O B E I S A N C E
M M C E B M C H A M B E R D O O R
```

Answers on page 191

"THE RAVEN" PT. 4

Every word listed is contained within the group of letters. Words can be found in a straight line horizontally, vertically, or diagonally. They may be read either forward or backward.

CROAKING

DISASTER

DOUBTLESS

FARTHER

FEATHER

FLOWN

FLUTTERED

GAUNT

LONELY

MELANCHOLY

MORROW

MUTTERED

OMINOUS BIRD

OUTPOUR

PLACID BUST

RAVEN

SAD SOUL

SPOKEN

STARTLED

STILLNESS

UNGAINLY

UNHAPPY

UTTERED

UTTERS

VELVET

WORD

```
T  H  E  R  N  F  S  T  I  L  L  N  E  S  S  A  V
E  N  W  A  S  E  F  P  I  R  R  E  H  T  R  A  F
R  M  S  T  P  A  K  U  L  B  L  U  I  S  D  H  E
L  U  D  I  N  T  T  O  H  A  Y  H  T  Y  E  N  G
U  T  O  G  D  H  G  V  P  P  C  U  V  T  R  M  O
O  T  C  P  Z  E  Y  Q  P  S  B  I  O  O  E  N  M
S  E  R  F  T  R  O  A  R  I  O  J  D  E  T  R  B
D  R  Y  I  V  U  H  W  L  J  E  Q  H  B  T  I  S
A  E  O  M  I  N  O  U  S  B  I  R  D  N  U  F  R
S  D  F  L  U  T  T  E  R  E  D  Y  U  B  L  S  E
D  O  U  B  T  L  E  S  S  A  M  A  R  O  U  J  T
D  Z  D  E  L  T  R  A  T  S  G  X  W  D  Y  P  S
W  O  R  R  O  M  G  H  O  E  O  N  R  I  O  R  A
L  R  N  J  Y  L  E  N  O  L  V  O  M  V  A  W  S
M  E  L  A  N  C  H  O  L  Y  W  L  F  V  K  P  I
G  N  I  K  A  O  R  C  V  P  K  H  E  F  M  C  D
U  N  G  A  I  N  L  Y  Y  Y  T  N  I  V  F  A  B
```

Answers on page 192

Every word listed is contained within the group of letters. Words can be found in a straight line horizontally, vertically, or diagonally. They may be read either forward or backward.

ANGELS	IMPLORE
ASHORE	LAMPLIGHT
BIRD	NEVERMORE
BURNED	PERFUMED
DESERT	PROPHET
DESOLATE	QUAFF
DEVIL	RECLINING
DIVINING	RESPITE
ENCHANTED	SWUNG
ENGAGED	SYLLABLE
FAINT	TEMPTER
FOWL	TINKLED
GLOATING	TOSSED

```
T  L  B  E  N  G  A  G  E  D  Z  D  E  S  E  R  T
B  Q  W  H  M  B  L  N  L  A  M  P  L  I  G  H  T
G  E  R  O  L  P  M  I  G  T  N  Z  S  L  E  F  T
N  L  G  G  F  J  D  H  S  E  W  Y  P  P  F  U  N
I  E  N  E  M  U  P  Y  G  R  L  W  T  A  E  J  I
T  R  I  G  E  I  Y  P  D  L  Z  S  U  R  T  H  A
A  O  N  N  I  R  V  B  A  T  Z  Q  N  E  A  D  F
O  H  I  I  T  D  O  B  U  R  N  E  D  T  L  E  W
L  S  L  N  F  E  L  M  C  T  Z  V  Z  P  O  M  I
G  A  C  I  U  E  H  M  R  W  J  R  I  M  S  U  K
W  A  E  V  H  K  R  P  D  E  B  D  T  E  E  F  D
L  C  R  I  U  G  S  G  O  G  V  I  E  T  D  R  P
J  J  F  D  H  T  U  T  Z  R  N  E  S  V  I  E  U
D  E  T  N  A  H  C  N  E  K  P  X  N  B  I  P  W
A  V  T  X  J  T  O  E  L  L  P  C  B  F  E  L  V
D  E  S  S  O  T  R  E  S  P  I  T  E  C  L  H  Y
P  K  W  B  C  W  D  P  J  G  N  U  W  S  I  C  I
```

Answers on page 192

"THE RAVEN" PT. 6

Every word listed is contained within the group of letters. Words can be found in a straight line horizontally, vertically, or diagonally. They may be read either forward or backward. Leftover letters will reveal an interesting bit of trivia about Poe's legend.

ADORE	NEVERMORE
ANGELS	PALLID
BENDS	PARTING
BIRD	PROPHET
CHAMBER	RADIANT
CLASP	RAVEN
DEMON	SHADOW
DEVIL	SIGN
DISTANT	SOUL
EVIL	SPOKEN
HEAVEN	STREAMING
LENORE	TEMPEST
LONELINESS	TOKEN

```
T S D N E B H E L R A N V E N D E
P W A G A V T S N E F I E R S R T
P A U I B N I L I E N S T K O I H
E D R S A I G L N T V O H M O B E
N E W T E M P E S T K A R Y O P R
K E S S I V E N L E I E R E S A S
N I O G M N I R N S V D R S R L O
D U R O N N J A E N U E A A L P
L S T R E A M I N G R N D M Y I R
2 9 1 8 V 4 5 U N D I I E R O D O
P O E S A P S E U L A L C D O N P
N Y M Q E P U A E N R H I L E S H
A L T H H S O N T U A G H V T H E
E P O E M A O B R M O U G H E T T
P O E F A L M E B I T D I D N D T
G I V E H C I E M A W A G E T O L
A D O R E I R V S H A D O W E O N
```

Hidden Message: _____

_____

Answers on page 192

THE TYLER ADMINISTRATION

Every word listed is contained within the group of letters. Words can be found in a straight line horizontally, vertically, or diagonally. They may be read either forward or backward.

ACCESSION

CONSTRUCTIONIST

CUSTOM HOUSE

HAPLESS

HENRY CLAY

INEPT

JOHN TYLER

NATIONAL BANK

OREGON

PACIFIC OCEAN

POCKET VETO

SAMUEL NELSON

TARIFFS

TENTH

VICE PRESIDENT

WHIG PARTY

WILLIAM HENRY HARRISON

```
E  K  A  T  H  L  J  T  G  G  S  K  E  P  W  D  T  M  H  Y  N
E  N  U  T  W  U  N  P  L  V  R  J  K  G  Q  F  N  K  P  P  O
M  U  Q  Y  A  L  C  Y  R  N  E  H  Q  Y  Q  I  E  J  Q  U  S
F  U  G  W  Y  R  I  T  V  V  B  N  X  K  P  D  D  H  C  A  I
W  A  Q  C  H  E  I  Y  K  E  U  J  C  M  B  E  I  V  F  S  R
I  Q  F  C  A  U  U  F  D  G  D  N  G  R  Z  E  S  N  Y  I  R
I  U  F  R  P  G  I  V  F  B  O  P  M  N  O  L  E  C  V  H  A
K  R  R  Q  L  G  A  S  H  S  S  E  U  T  E  T  R  O  T  E  H
R  N  V  Q  E  A  G  I  L  Y  J  I  E  Y  S  F  P  N  N  P  Y
J  P  A  R  S  F  W  E  H  X  Y  V  D  T  U  K  E  S  O  A  R
Z  N  H  B  S  J  N  E  I  Z  T  W  M  R  O  T  C  T  I  C  N
S  U  G  T  L  L  O  L  T  E  L  H  J  A  H  W  I  R  S  I  E
O  K  Q  H  E  A  R  Q  K  R  E  L  M  P  M  T  V  U  S  F  H
X  L  I  U  G  F  N  C  W  E  H  Q  V  G  O  B  C  C  E  I  M
O  X  M  V  E  W  O  O  F  L  A  Q  H  I  T  Q  D  T  C  C  A
C  A  A  W  Z  P  M  N  I  Y  L  R  H  H  S  A  L  I  C  O  I
S  F  K  V  R  H  R  O  W  T  F  N  H  W  U  M  N  O  A  C  L
O  P  H  K  G  L  N  G  Z  N  A  Z  B  E  C  E  T  N  M  E  L
R  S  D  M  Z  D  B  E  B  H  A  N  P  B  P  X  V  I  J  A  I
N  R  Y  C  X  V  B  R  K  O  N  T  D  T  T  Y  I  S  H  N  W
P  N  C  P  X  V  L  O  O  J  L  W  D  X  H  Y  F  T  J  D  C
```

Answers on page 192

171

ANSWERS

Edgar Allan Poe
(Pages 4-5)

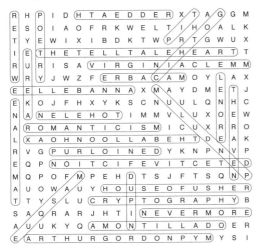

The Poe Family
(Pages 8-9)

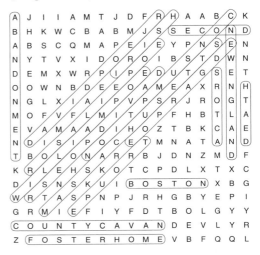

Themes and Genres
(Pages 6-7)

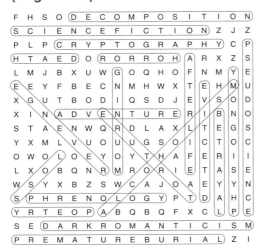

William Henry Leonard Poe
(Pages 10-11)

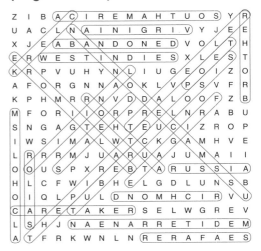

ANSWERS

Elizabeth Arnold Hopkins Poe
(Pages 12-13)

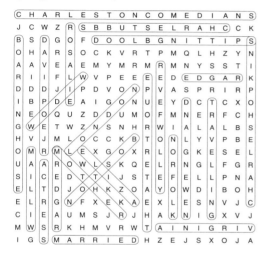

David Poe Jr.
(Pages 14-15)

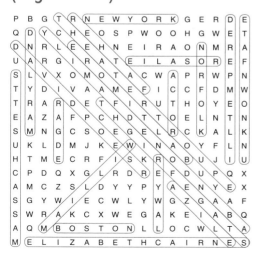

Virginia Eliza Clemm Poe
(Pages 16-17)

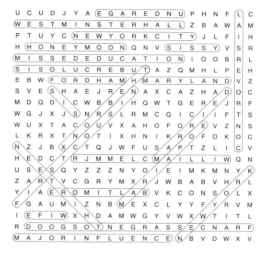

Poe's Upbringing With the Allans
(Pages 18-19)

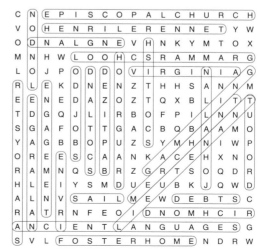

ANSWERS

Poe's Military Career
(Pages 20-21)

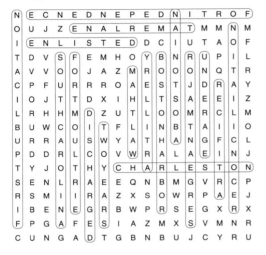

Poe's Publishers
(Pages 24-25)

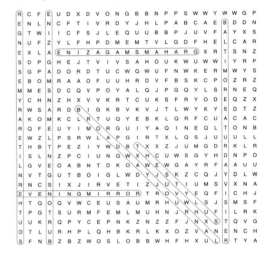

Poe's Discharge From the Military
(Pages 22-23)

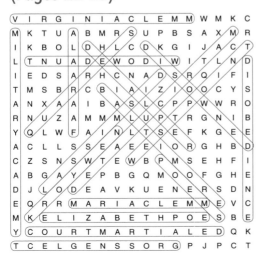

Poe's Writing Career
(Pages 26-27)

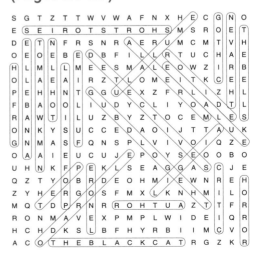

ANSWERS

Poe's Poetry
(Pages 28-29)

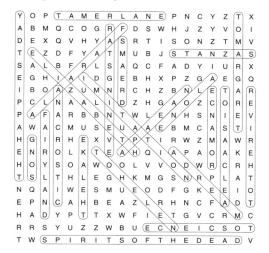

Poe's Tales
(Pages 32-33)

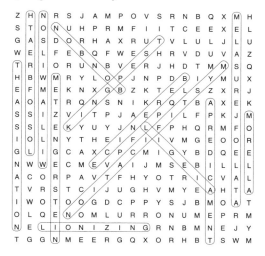

Poe's Poetry Pt. 2
(Pages 30-31)

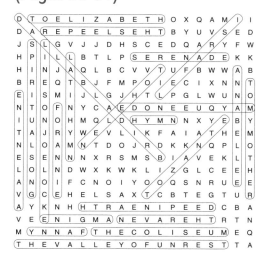

Poe's Tales Pt. 2
(Pages 34-35)

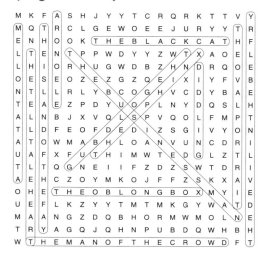

ANSWERS

Poe's Tales Pt. 3
(Pages 36-37)

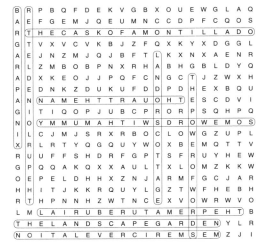

Poe's Agony
(Pages 38-39)

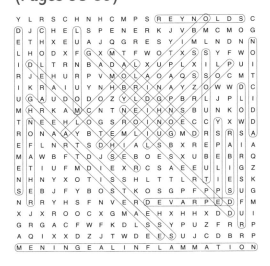

"The Purloined Letter"
(Pages 40-41)

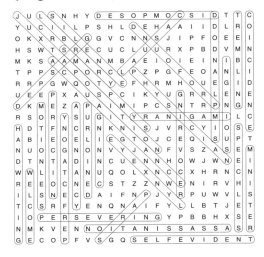

"The Purloined Letter" Pt. 2
(Pages 42-43)

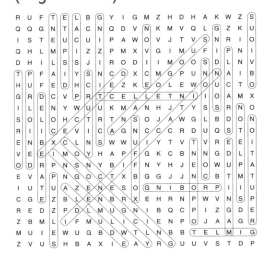

ANSWERS

"The Premature Burial"
(Pages 44-45)

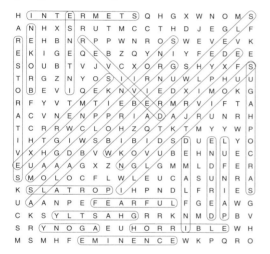

"The Premature Burial" Pt. 2
(Pages 46-47)

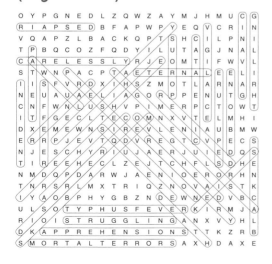

"The Haunted Palace" Pt. 1
(Pages 48-49)

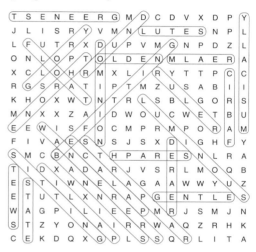

"The Haunted Palace" Pt. 2
(Pages 50-51)

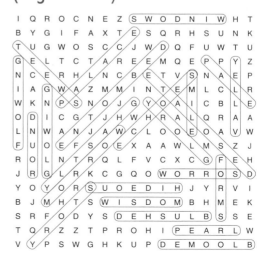

ANSWERS

"The Conqueror Worm" Pt. 1
(Pages 52-53)

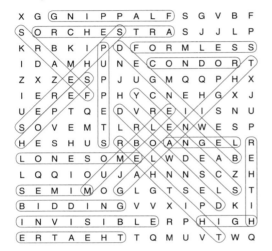

"To One in Paradise"
(Pages 56-57)

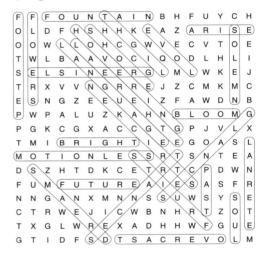

"The Conqueror Worm" Pt. 2
(Pages 54-55)

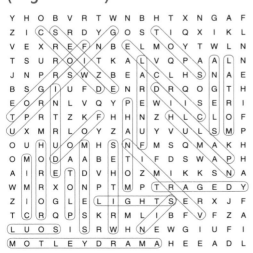

"The City in the Sea" Pt. 1
(Pages 58-59)

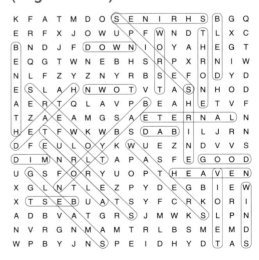

ANSWERS

"The City in the Sea" Pt. 2
(Pages 60-61)

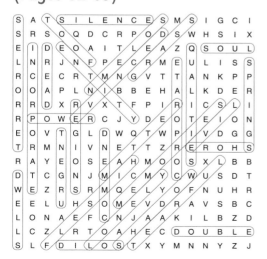

"Silence"
(Pages 62-63)

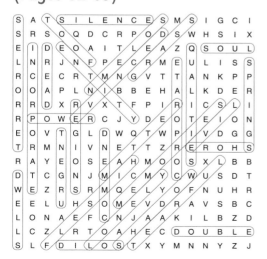

"Dream-Land" Pt. 1
(Pages 64-65)

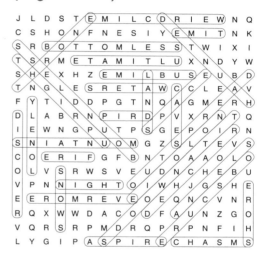

"Dream-Land" Pt. 2
(Pages 66-67)

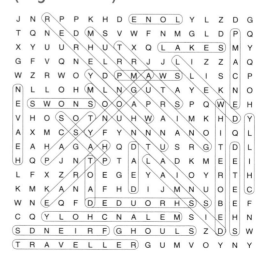

ANSWERS

"Dream-Land" Pt. 3 (Pages 68-69)

Hidden message: "Dream-Land" was 1st published in 1844 in *Graham's Magazine*.

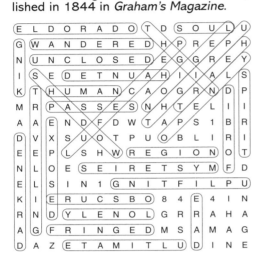

"The Tell-Tale Heart" Pt. 1 (Pages 72-73)

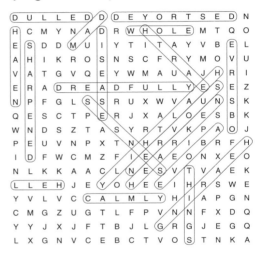

"A Dream Within a Dream" (Pages 70-71)

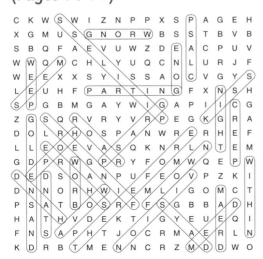

"The Tell-Tale Heart" Pt. 2 (Pages 74-75)

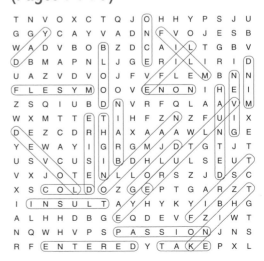

ANSWERS

"The Tell-Tale Heart" Pt. 3
(Pages 76-77)

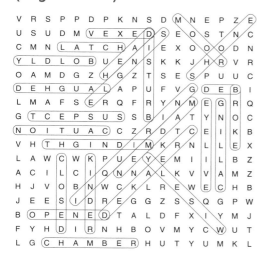

"The Tell-Tale Heart" Pt. 5
(Pages 80-81)

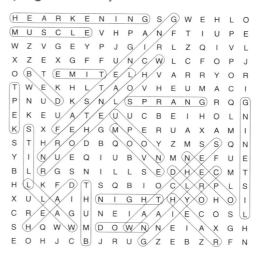

"The Tell-Tale Heart" Pt. 4
(Pages 78-79)

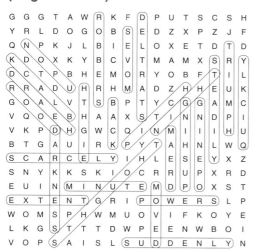

"The Tell-Tale Heart" Pt. 6
(Pages 82-83)

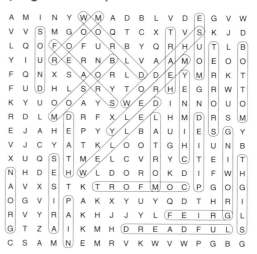

ANSWERS

"The Tell-Tale Heart" Pt. 7
(Pages 84-85)

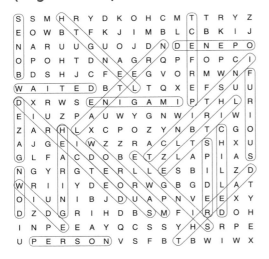

"The Tell-Tale Heart" Pt. 8
(Pages 86-87)

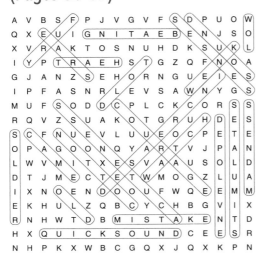

"The Tell-Tale Heart" Pt. 9
(Pages 88-89)

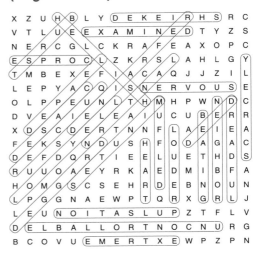

"The Tell-Tale Heart" Pt. 10
(Pages 90-91)

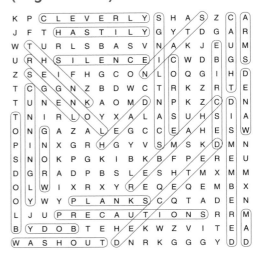

ANSWERS

"The Tell-Tale Heart" Pt. 11 (Pages 92-93)

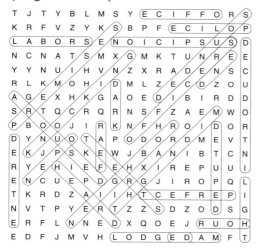

"The Tell-Tale Heart" Pt. 13 (Pages 96-97)

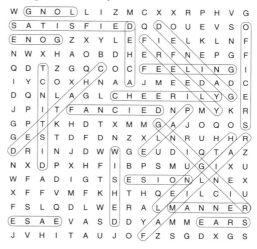

"The Tell-Tale Heart" Pt. 12 (Pages 94-95)

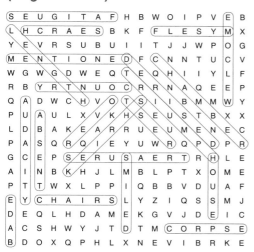

"The Tell-Tale Heart" Pt. 14 (Pages 98-99)

Hidden Message: "The Tell-Tale Heart" was first published in January of 1843 in the short-lived Boston magazine named *The Pioneer.* Poe was most likely paid only ten dollars for the gothic fiction tale.

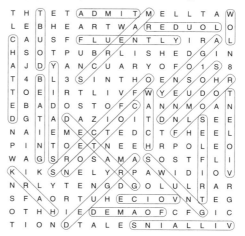

ANSWERS

"The Black Cat" Pt. 1
(Pages 100-101)

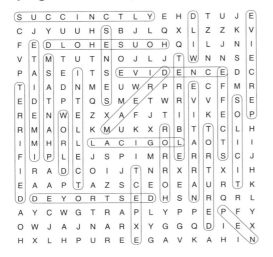

"The Black Cat" Pt. 3
(Pages 104-105)

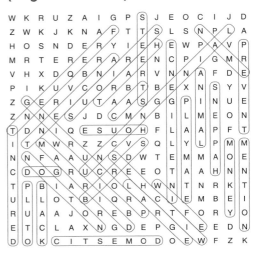

"The Black Cat" Pt. 2
(Pages 102-103)

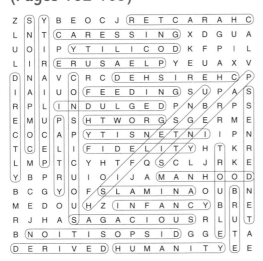

"The Black Cat" Pt. 4
(Pages 106-107)

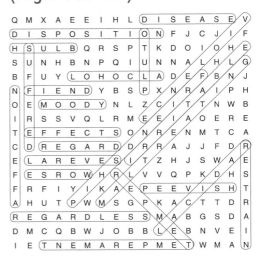

ANSWERS

"The Black Cat" Pt. 5
(Pages 108-109)

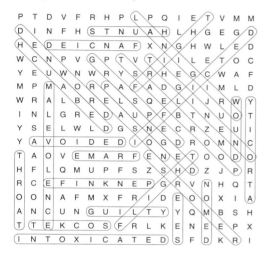

"The Black Cat" Pt. 6
(Pages 110-111)

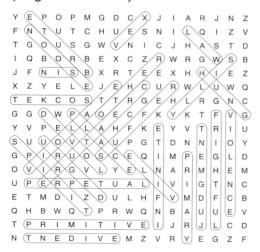

"The Black Cat" Pt. 7
(Pages 112-113)

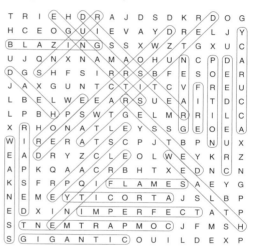

"The Black Cat" Pt. 8
(Pages 114-115)

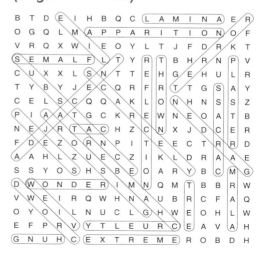

ANSWERS

"The Black Cat" Pt. 9
(Pages 116-117)

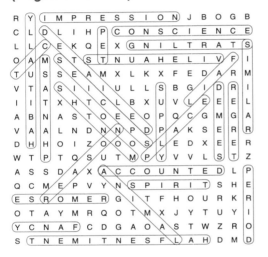

"The Black Cat" Pt. 11
(Pages 120-121)

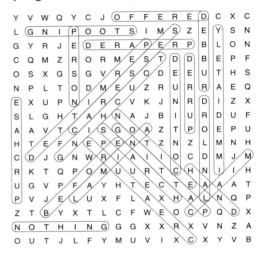

"The Black Cat" Pt. 10
(Pages 118-119)

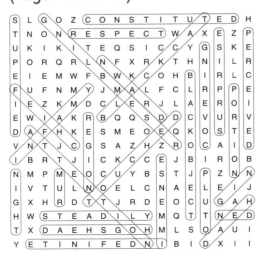

"The Black Cat" Pt. 12
(Pages 122-123)

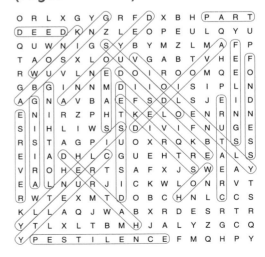

ANSWERS

"The Black Cat" Pt. 13
(Pages 124-125)

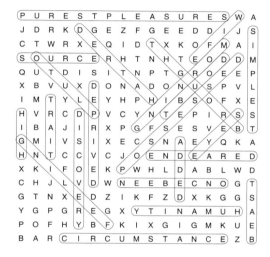

"The Black Cat" Pt. 15
(Pages 128-129)

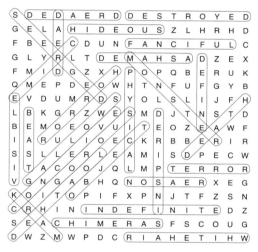

"The Black Cat" Pt. 14
(Pages 126-127)

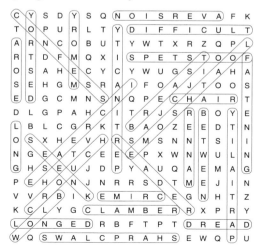

"The Black Cat" Pt. 16
(Pages 130-131)

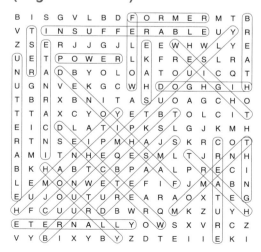

ANSWERS

"The Black Cat" Pt. 17
(Pages 132-133)

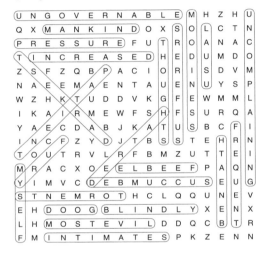

"The Black Cat" Pt. 18
(Pages 134-135)

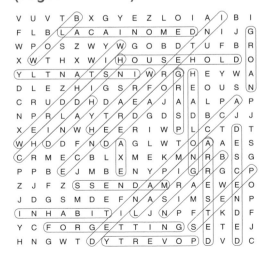

"The Black Cat" Pt. 19
(Pages 136-137)

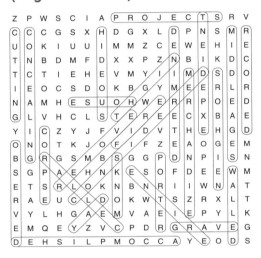

"The Black Cat" Pt. 20
(Pages 138-139)

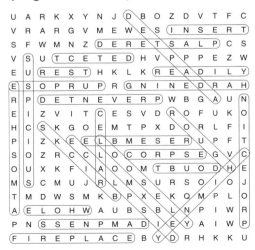

ANSWERS

"The Black Cat" Pt. 21
(Pages 140-141)

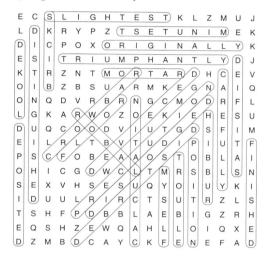

"The Black Cat" Pt. 23
(Pages 144-145)

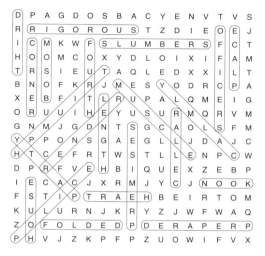

"The Black Cat" Pt. 22
(Pages 142-143)

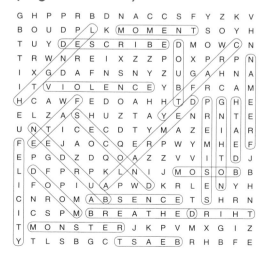

"The Black Cat" Pt. 24
(Pages 146-147)

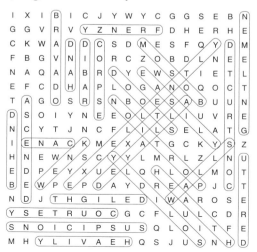

ANSWERS

"The Black Cat" Pt. 25 (Pages 148-149)

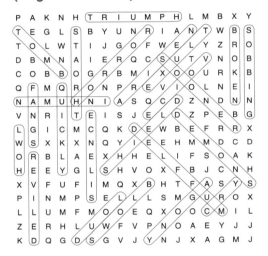

"The Black Cat" Pt. 26 (Pages 150-151)

Hidden Message: "The Black Cat" was first published in the *Saturday Evening Post* on August 19, 1843. The story has been parodied and adapted many times.

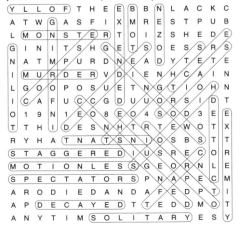

"Sonnet—To Science" (Pages 152-153)

Hidden Message: "Sonnet—To Science" was published in Poe's second of poetry, *Al Aaraaf*, in 1829, which was the first publication that Poe didn't use the pen name 'a Bostonian.'

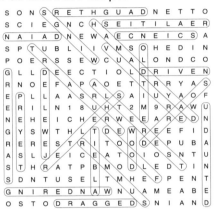

"A Dream" (Pages 154-155)

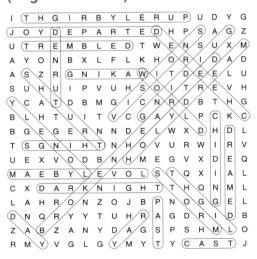

ANSWERS

"Eldorado" (Pages 156-157)

Hidden Message: "Eldorado" was first published in a Boston weekly on April 21, 1849. Concurrent with the California Goldrush, the poem recounts the lost mythical native-Colombian city made of all gold.

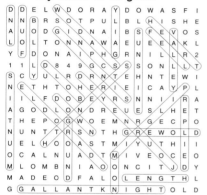

"The Raven" Pt. 1 (Pages 158-159)

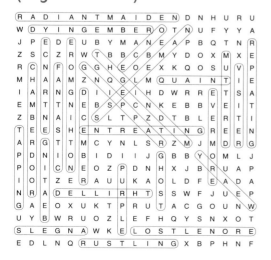

"The Raven" Pt. 2 (Pages 160-161)

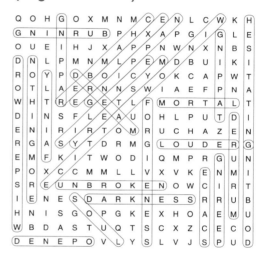

"The Raven" Pt. 3 (Pages 162-163)

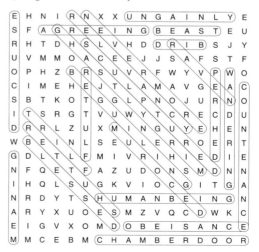

ANSWERS

"The Raven" Pt. 4
(Pages 164-165)

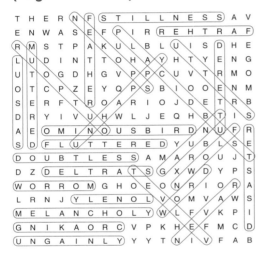

"The Raven" Pt. 5
(Pages 166-167)

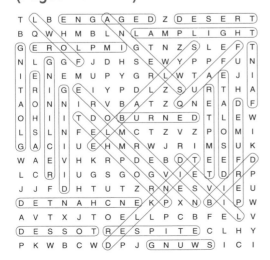

"The Raven" Pt. 6 (Pages 168-169)

Hidden Message: "The Raven" was first published in the *New York Evening Mirror* on January 29, 1845, under Poe's pseudonym "Quarles." Although the poem brought Poe fame, it didn't give him a wage to live on.

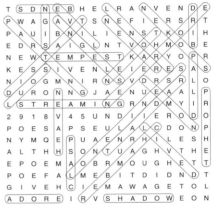

The Tyler Administration
(Pages 170-171)

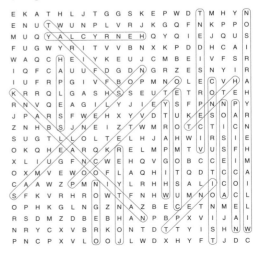